ALSO BY SHARIE KOHLER

Night Falls on the Wicked
My Soul to Keep
To Crave a Blood Moon
Kiss of a Dark Moon
Marked by Moonlight

Haunted by Your Touch
(with Jeaniene Frost and Shayla Black)

SHARIE KOHLER

A SOUL SO WICKED

POCKET BOOKS

New York   London   Toronto   Sydney   New Delhi

Pocket Books
A Division of Simon & Schuster, Inc.
1230 Avenue of the Americas
New York, NY 10020

First Pocket Books paperback edition January 2013

POCKET and colophon are registered trademarks of Simon & Schuster, Inc.

For information about special discounts for bulk purchases, please contact Simon & Schuster Special Sales at 1-866-506-1949 or business@simonandschuster.com.

The Simon & Schuster Speakers Bureau can bring authors to your live event. For more information or to book an event, contact the Simon & Schuster Speakers Bureau at 1-866-248-3049 or visit our website at www.simonspeakers.com.

Manufactured in the United States of America

10   9   8   7   6   5   4   3   2   1

ISBN: 978-1-5011-0706-1
ISBN: 978-1-4516-1144-1 (ebook)

To Jared, for loving this series.
And because I love you . . .

A SOUL SO WICKED

PROLOGUE

70 AD

Pain shuddered through her body, as steady and unrelenting as the ocean waves that had pounded the shores of her girlhood home. How she longed for those days of innocence now. Pain-free days when she floated through life beneath anyone's notice. Before *this*.

She swallowed and fought back against the rolling tide of nausea. Forcing her eyes open, she flattened her hands on the floor and tried to lift her head, but the boot at the center of her back held her pinned.

She shook the dark hair from her eyes, gasping as the heel ground into her spine. Her head dropped back down; her cheek crushed into the gritty floor.

Her eyes wide and aching, too terrified too weep, she stretched her arm across the packed-dirt floor for her husband, desperate to reach him.

Like a circling vulture, Lord Marshan walked lazily about Michel, his fine boots, polished to a high shine, thudding with each step.

She looked up at his face. He used a handkerchief to dab at the bloody scratches she'd left on his cheek.

"I don't ask much from my people," he murmured, his voice deceptively gentle as he spread his arms wide with a flourish. "I'm known throughout this land for my generosity." He stopped an inch from Michel's head, his cold stare fixed down on her. "Respect. Loyalty. *Obedience*." His lips curled back from his teeth.

His dead eyes. The menace of that sneer. She felt her fate settle like a noose about her neck.

Now the tears came, rolling silently.

This was her fault. She had done this. She had put her family in danger. She choked back a sob and strained, still trying to reach her husband, frantic to touch him, as though she might somehow protect him with the merest brush of her hand.

Michel's head moved in the barest shake. What was he trying to convey? That she shouldn't move? Shouldn't speak?

Her grandmother wept in the corner, tears flowing down the weathered lines of her face as she pleaded, "Please, my lord! We meant no disrespect."

Marshan sent her a scathing glance and sighed, motioning to one of his men with a flick of his fingers. "Silence the hag, would you?"

One of the soldiers pulled back his fist and struck Grandmère. She slumped where she had huddled by the hearth, her small body as limp as a rag doll.

Tresa had denied Marshan what he wanted: *her*. She swallowed against the bitter scald of tears. He was lord and master. No one refused him. She should have just let him have his way and said nothing to Michel. It would be over and done with by now, and her family would be safe.

Only she had resisted his every overture for months now. When he'd come this afternoon and tried to collect more than his wife's herbs from her, she'd fought him. Struck him as if he were the lowliest peasant.

She closed her eyes in agony, reliving the moment when Michel and Grandmère had returned, walking in on Marshan as he shoved her down to the bed, tearing the clothes from her body.

If she hadn't fought, he would have been finished with her and gone. Instead Michel had attacked him. This was all her fault.

"Please," she begged. "I'm sorry. I'll do whatever you ask."

"Tresa," Michel admonished from where he lay in a broken heap, his voice a sharp rasp.

"Please, what?" Marshan bent and leveled his gaze on her. "Forget the fact that this peasant laid his filthy hands on me?" He swung his gaze to Michel. "Did you think you could touch me, carpenter?" He pulled back his leg and kicked her husband in the face.

She screamed at the crunch of bone, at the spurt of blood from his nose. Michel moaned, spitting out blood.

"He was just defending me," she cried out, struggling against the boot holding her in place.

"Defending you? And what *are* you, sorceress?"

She winced. There was far too much truth in the accusation.

Marshan whirled around and shoved the soldier off her. He pulled her up by her hair and shook her, his grip so tight she was surprised the strands didn't rip clean from her scalp. "How many innocents have you killed with your potions and wicked spells?"

She whimpered, grabbing his hand that gripped a fistful of hair. "I only heal," she panted. "Even your wife uses my poultices. Ask her!"

"What was that, witch?" He pushed his face closer to hers. So close she could smell the rancid garlic on his breath. "A threat against my lady wife?"

Icy dread washed over her. "No! I did not say that!"

He scanned the room, looking at each of his soldiers. "Did you hear that, men? Your queen has been threatened." He returned his gaze to her, and the absolute evil there wrapped her in its embrace.

"Burn the house," he announced in a calm voice, as if he were requesting lamb for dinner. His gaze flicked to her husband and grandmother. "Leave them in it."

"No!" She surged wildly from his grip with no thought to the strands that tore from her scalp. Michel and Grandmère were in no condition to save themselves. Not that they could defend themselves against Marshan and his knights even when able-bodied. There were simply too many of them.

She stomped down on Marshan's foot and his grip loosened. For a brief moment she reached Michel, held his battered face in her hands. Her vision blurred, overrun with tears. She flexed her fingers against his ravaged face, savoring, memorizing the feel of him. Blinking

fiercely, she whispered frantic words of love . . .
apologies . . . farewell . . .

He shook his head at her, his dark eyes
so full of pain and anguish. He covered her
hand against his cheek with one of his work-
roughened ones as though he could keep hold
of her there against him. The gesture felt so
tender and sweetly familiar that it made her
chest ache, knowing this was the last time she
would ever have that.

A knight grabbed her and started to pull her
away. She lurched forward and pressed a final
kiss to Michel's lips.

The knight came for her again, ready to
tear her away, and something swelled inside
her. The old frightening, overwhelming energy
expanded from deep in her core. Her muscles
buzzed from the power of it. She hadn't felt it
in years. Not since childhood. Not since she'd
learned to suppress it. To ignore it. Fight it.

The moment before he reached her, his body
lifted off the ground and launched through the
air. He landed with a crash across the room.
Everyone looked from him to her, their expressions a mixture of wonder and horror.

Her chest heaved with violent breaths. And
then they were on her, too many to fight. Even
if she could use her power, it was a wild, elusive

thing. Impossible to control, to summon. She didn't know how to harness it. She'd only ever denied it.

Still, she struggled, her feet thrashing off the ground as she watched Marshan's men lift the candles off her table and hold them to the curtain surrounding her bed. One soldier stood on a stool and lit the thatched rooftop. It immediately caught fire and sparks popped and rained down on them.

"Want us to leave her in here, too, my lord?"

"She's a witch," Marshan announced, his words as cold and unfeeling as his gaze. "Witches are drowned."

The words shot ice down her spine. It was the fate her parents and Grandmère had always feared for her. Why they had taught her to deny her *gift*.

Michel moaned and tried to stand, but a soldier kicked him back to the ground. Tresa tried to use her feet as she was dragged out of the house without her family.

"Michel!" She strained for a glimpse of him as she was carried away. Thick smoke already filled the cottage. Outside, the acrid smell hung thick, mingling with the aroma of wood fire and the villagers' brewing stews and baking breads.

In the fading light of dusk, a crowd gathered to watch, their faces cast in the red glow as they forgot about their dinners. None moved to help as she was dragged through the village and toward the river in her torn dress, parts of her exposed to every man's greedy eye.

Villagers trailed them. From somewhere in the crowd the cry of *witch* was taken up. She looked back toward the village, obscured now by a thick veil of trees. A dark, winding snake of smoke stretched into the sky. Even from the river, the sharp smell of her burning cottage filled her nose. It was all she could see in her mind. *Michel. Grandmère.*

At the river's edge, heavy chains were hastily wrapped around her. Several bone-breaking stones hung from the ends, weighing the chains so that they cut into her flesh.

She heard Marshan's voice over the crowd, pronouncing her guilty of various crimes, but she could only stare numbly at the sky, the dark curling serpent of smoke reaching high.

She lifted her face and closed her eyes. *Michel, I love you.*

A sudden warm breeze washed over her. She opened her eyes, watching as a dark shadow wended its way through the crowd toward her, ribboning through all the oblivious spectators.

Over and around bodies, like a lover's hand, it slid toward her.

It wasn't the first time shadows had visited her. Ever since she was a girl and had become aware of her *gift*—her ability to move things with just a thought—the shadows had plagued her. Tempting her, offering her promises of power and eternal life in exchange for her soul.

She'd resisted the demons' dark lure, discovering that the more she suppressed her magic, the less they appeared to tempt her.

Despair twisted inside her heart. For all her efforts, Michel and Grandmère were dead, their flesh and blood reducing to ashes as she stood waiting for her murder at the river's edge.

Marshan's men shoved her forward. The shadow reached her just as her feet met the water.

"Be gone, demon," she hissed, wincing at the cold water lapping her toes.

The demon ignored her, wrapping around her like a warm blanket, seductively soothing. Its guttural voice curled enticingly in her ear.

Wouldn't you like to make him pay? Make him suffer for Michel's death . . . make him know Michel's pain? Your pain . . .

She shook her head, her hair tossing wildly. In her mind, she heard Grandmère's voice as she had all her life, warning her to resist the shadows.

"No!" she shouted, denying more than this demon. Denying her death, the death of her family—the loss of everything that mattered in her world.

A pair of soldiers dragged her out deeper into the water, until her feet couldn't touch. The only thing keeping her afloat was their hard hands. The weight of the chains pulled on her bones, sucked her body down.

And what of your grandmother? Did her old, tired bones deserve the fire? She woke, you know. At the first lick of flames. Marshan should pay. He shouldn't be allowed to live on to inflict further pain.

The demon's words arrowed straight to her bleeding heart.

Her chin bobbed at the water's surface. With the weight of chains and stones, she'd sink right down. Plunge in this very spot to a watery grave.

Water slapped against her lips. "Please," she sobbed, but she was no longer sure who she was begging. Marshan and his men? Or the demon propositioning her?

The hands released her and she sank with the demon's voice a whispery coax in her ear.

Come, Tresa . . . don't let your death go unavenged.

The air left her in the roar of a thousand bubbles, and then there was no more. Cold, brackish water rushed inside her mouth and nose, filling her lungs. The water was dark. Her eyes could see nothing as she thrashed, desperate for air, for freedom. Life.

Come, Tresa. Avenge Michel . . .

Her lungs burned. Spots flashed before her eyes, brightening her dark, dying world.

Avenge Michel . . .

The words spun dizzily in her head, eclipsing all else. Marshan had to pay. This was her only thought as her hair rippled like silky seaweed around her.

Suddenly the words formed in her head, exploding free.

Curse Marshan! Make him pay. Make him pay and I am yours. Demon, I am yours . . .

ONE

The only beautiful thing in the world whose beauty lasts forever is a pure, fair soul.

—Bram Stoker

PRESENT DAY

Darius's footsteps echoed off the silent street. The waning moon gleamed down, casting the dark street in a pearly glow. He inhaled, glad that he didn't need to worry about another full moon for nearly a month. He hated losing those three nights, putting his mission on pause, but he could do nothing about it.

At least not yet.

For now, this was the life he lived. As much as he despised it, he could only make the best of it. That's what he had been doing, but finally he was close. After all these years, the witch would evade him no longer. He'd have her—and an end to the curse.

He stopped before the narrow brick town house and double-checked the slip of paper in his pocket to make sure he was at the right place. He couldn't very well meet with the FBI analyst in her field office, but he was surprised she'd given him her home address. He could be anyone . . . a dangerous man. A *beast*. There were all manner of predators in this world.

He pushed the buzzer and waited. A yippy dog inside immediately started up a frenzy of barking. Through the blurry stained-glass front door he watched the vague shape of a female appear, scooping up the dog in her arms. A pile of dark hair bobbed on top of her head as she approached.

She unbolted the door and peered at him over the wide rims of her glasses. "Darius?"

He nodded. "Anna Posner?"

She stood on her tiptoes and looked over his shoulder, evidently assuring herself that he was alone.

Satisfied, she undid the flimsy chain and motioned him inside. The fluffy white dog growled low in its throat, shaking uncontrollably in its mistress's arms.

"Hush, Lacy." She sent Darius an apologetic look as she patted the dog's head. "She's usually very friendly."

"No problem." The dog had good instincts. It recognized him for what he was. The same could not be said for Anna Posner.

They lingered in the small foyer. The analyst stared at him with a rather transfixed expression on her face . . . as if she'd never had a man in her home before and didn't quite know what to do. He eyed her baggy sweatshirt and sweatpants that hid any hint of her gender.

"Do you have the information I need?" he asked, eager to get what he came for and leave. He wasn't one for banter.

She blinked, straightening to all of her diminutive height. "Uh. Yes. Sure. Wasn't easy, of course. A first name and the little description you provided isn't much to go on . . . especially as off the grid as this woman happens to be."

Of course she was off the grid, or he would have found her sooner. "So you located her?"

"Naturally." She blinked like he'd asked the silliest of questions. "That's what I do." She gestured for him to follow her.

He trailed her a few feet down the corridor into her home office. She immediately took a seat at her desk, behind her computer, setting her growling dog in her lap. She tapped at a few keys with rapid-fire speed.

"I think this is her . . ." The printer began spitting out a sheet of paper, which she pulled out and handed to him.

He glanced at the fuzzy image: a slim female, dark hair peeping out from the hood of a coat.

From the accounts he'd heard, it could be her. But so could a lot of other women.

He stared at the blurry image awhile longer, absorbing everything he could. There was something about the female. A way she held herself even when she didn't know someone was looking. A guardedness.

"Where is she?"

"That was taken at a small airport in Rocksburgh ten months ago."

"Ten *months* ago?" She could be anywhere now.

With several more clicks of the keyboard, she printed out another page. "Here." She tapped a small town on a map of Alaska. "This town is an hour's drive from Anchorage. I found the name of a Tresa King on a roster for a town meeting, signed two weeks ago. Tresa's not the most common name."

Two weeks ago. He stared at the small dot on the map, his chest filling with hope. A town meeting? Would she be participating in society? Something as mundane as a town meeting? It didn't fit with his idea of her, but then, she wasn't operating under her own free will. She was a slave to something else.

He folded the second printout and tucked it inside his jacket. From his other pocket, he pulled out the payment owed and dropped it onto her desk.

She opened the envelope and peered inside. "Thanks." Rising, she led him to the door. "Let me know if you ever need any more work done."

"A word of advice."

She gazed at him, her eyes wide through her smudged lenses.

"If you're going to freelance, don't be so trusting. Don't invite your clientele inside your home."

She blinked up at him. "You mean I shouldn't have trusted you?" she asked baldly, trying to smile, but it failed to reach her eyes.

"No," he returned evenly, grasping the doorknob. "You shouldn't have. You never know what kind of man you're dealing with . . . especially after he gets what he wants from you. Once you become unnecessary, you're expendable."

The pulse at her neck beat faster, like that of a rabbit face-to-face with its hunter. His gaze narrowed on the rapidly thrumming flesh, everything in him pulling tight. Humans. So very fragile. So tempting.

She looked nervous now, but he could smell her excitement, too. An acrid, loamy aroma on the air. She was getting her kicks off the danger of this moment.

"And what kind of man are you?" she asked.

He leaned in closer; whispered the word against her ear as he inhaled her. Citrus shampoo and popcorn. "A killer."

At first disbelief crossed her face, but as he continued to stare at her, her expression changed to trepidation. Her hand moved to her throat self-consciously and she edged back a step.

Satisfied that she would be more cautious in the future, he turned to go. Perhaps he shouldn't have bothered to warn her, but he couldn't help caring. A weakness maybe, but caring was what made him different from his brethren—bloodthirsty animals. As long as he cared, deep in his gut he didn't feel like he was a total lost cause.

Descending the steps of her town house, he vanished into the night, moving quickly, nothing more than a shadow to any passing eye. He covered several blocks, passing a row of sleepy bungalows in a newly restored section of Charlottesville. Restored or not, there was no hiding the fact that three blocks away was one of the most dangerous areas of the city. A slum where all manner of unsavory characters skulked.

He had once loved places like this. They were familiar . . . the best hunting grounds.

At first he thought the men trailing him were thugs who had drifted over in search of prey among the quiet, trimmed lawns. He walked on, unconcerned, as he waited for them to make their move. It wasn't a question of him being ready. He was always ready. He was a creature of instinct, his aggression and his violent impulses always there, simmering just beneath the surface.

As they continued to trail him, following him out of the neighborhood and into a wide parking lot of cracked and broken asphalt that backed into a strip of warehouses deserted for the night, he concluded they might be more than your standard thugs.

He stopped. Without turning around, he called out, "Are we going to do this all night?"

The footsteps stopped. The hush of silence fell. He knew human nature. At his invitation, the thugs would either run or attack.

Only neither happened.

Quiet surrounded him.

His skin prickled and pulled tight. Even without a full moon, his strength and speed put him at an advantage. All of his senses sharpened. He listened, straining for the slightest sounds that were unnatural to the surroundings. And then he heard the faintest click.

He dropped to the ground effortlessly in one liquid motion as the bullet whizzed above him. He scanned the parking lot and spotted the figure in the distance, taking aim again.

Darius moved then, unleashing himself. He covered the distance separating him and his would-be killer in one second and snatched the gun from the man's hands. The man flailed and writhed, cursing, striking him with useless blows.

Darius's nostrils flared. He brought the pistol closer to his nose and inhaled the sweet, metallic odor. *Silver*. Kryptonite for him and his kind. His gaze snapped back to the man, and he understood instantly who—*what*—he was. "Hunter," he spat.

"And you're Darius," the guy sneered, his lip curling over his teeth. He grimaced when Darius tightened his hold around his throat.

"How'd you find me?" He'd worked hard to stay off the grid.

"You're on every hunter's wish list—the lycan without a pack. You should have been taken out years ago."

Darius didn't bother responding. How could he explain that he was different from the rest of the lycans out there? The hunter wouldn't believe him. He scoured the area for more hunters. Where there was one, there were others.

Almost on cue, a dark SUV tore into the lot at full speed. The vehicle jerked to a stop several feet before them, trapping them within the bright glare of headlights. Singed rubber polluted the air.

Darius positioned the hunter in front of him, not keen on taking a silver bullet. The other hunters spilled out of the SUV. Using the doors for cover, they sized up Darius and the captive hunter.

"Sam, you okay?" one barked out.

"Let him go!" another shouted.

Darius smiled lazily, considering the scenario. Four hunters, all with weapons aimed at him. He'd faced worse odds.

"I'd be happy to let you all go. If you just walk away and forget you ever saw me."

"Not a chance in hell!"

Darius sighed. He didn't relish killing anyone, even hunters. They thought they were doing the right thing. Truthfully, most lycans needed killing. They killed indiscriminately, gorging themselves every full moon. Like rabid dogs, they needed to be put down.

Sam squirmed in his grasp, his efforts wasted. The slightest squeeze and Darius could put an end to him. Years ago, he would have. Before he'd regained his conscience.

"How'd you find me?" he pressed, tightening his grip on Sam's throat. For years, he'd been mere myth and legend. He'd like to know how his existence had been verified, how he'd suddenly made it onto every hunter's kill list. It was a mistake he wouldn't make again.

"You've been getting a lot of exposure lately. Heard you've been working with some kill-for-hires—and a bunch of scientists," Sam panted. "Did you think you could hide from us? We've got men everywhere."

He shouldn't have been surprised. Single-minded in his focus, he'd cast his usual caution aside and gotten sloppy in his quest to break his curse. Hiring dozens of researchers, historians, and even his own army to accompany him on certain missions wasn't exactly keeping a low profile.

He couldn't regret it, though. The prey he hunted wasn't anything he'd ever faced before. He didn't know what to expect, but he had to defeat her. For himself. For the world.

"I don't know what you've been playing at, *dog,* but you've lived long enough. Time to give it up."

He sighed. He'd played enough with these

hunters, who smelled of the silver they packed. "Five of you? You really should have brought more—"

He flung Sam toward his comrades in a swift shove. Before anyone could register what had just happened, he catapulted into the air, touching down on top of the SUV before springing through the air and landing in the parking lot. He rushed across the asphalt, a blur in the night, too fast for the eye to process. Bullets plugged the air around him.

He stopped moments later, several miles away. The night hummed around him, silent except for the distant growl of cars on the far-off highway.

Sliding his hands into his pockets, he was comforted by the crinkle of paper there. That was all that mattered. Whistling softly, he strode down the sidewalk.

In the marrow of his bones, he knew he was closing in—he felt it. He'd have her this time. Whether or not he reclaimed his soul in the process, he'd finally have her.

He'd have justice.

TWO

Her face is lovely in her utter stillness. Possibly lovelier than the other two. Air falls in hot rasps from your lips. It's impossible to resist. You have to touch her. Just a slide of your fingertips against her cheek, her throat, the delicate shape of her collarbone.

Envy fills you . . . deep and dark, a covetous yearning that pools in all those hollow places inside, every nook and cranny, until you're overflowing, ready to burst.

You reach for the bag and spread rose petals around her gentle curves, taking care to crush a few of the petals so their aroma curls on the air. So romantic.

In your other hand—the knife.

It feels comfortable. Right. Like it belongs there.

You give her cheek a sharp little slap, trying to rouse her. No sense in doing this if she isn't awake to appreciate it.

She moans, a catlike little mewl, and you can't help wondering if she makes that sound when she makes love, too. When she's with him. The very possibility consumes you, smolders hotly in your blood until your breath falls fast and hard. Eager for it, you slap her harder.

Her eyes flutter open, and it's there in that glimmering brown—her absolute wonder and awe as she sees you. You press the knife to her supple flesh and understanding floods her face. She knows.

She's ready.

At last.

Now you can begin.

TRESA WOKE WITH A gasp, a scream lodged in her throat. She clutched the bedcovers to her heaving chest, staring blindly at the wall, straight ahead at the picture of a sandy beach dotted with striped umbrellas. She blinked, trying to focus on the seascape and rid herself of the image of a dying girl.

But the horrible images clung, impossible to shake. Just like the other dreams. They were becoming a regular occurrence.

It surprised her that mere dreams should take such a hold on her and fill her with such horror. She had lived through countless terrible things and those images haunted her every time she closed her eyes. Even though the memories were faint and gray, she struggled to suppress the fuzzy recollections so that they didn't overwhelm and cripple her.

But this dream was fresh, frighteningly clear. Just like the others, it felt . . . real. Like it wasn't even a nightmare. The aroma of roses still teased her nose.

She dragged a hand over her face and closed her eyes in a slow blink. The girl's face was waiting, the brown eyes rising up in the dark of her mind. Tresa quickly reopened her eyes.

The girl's fear, her terror and pain . . . the person wielding the knife had relished every moment.

She flung back her covers and stepped into her slippers. Walking from her bedroom, she flipped on the kitchen light and squinted in the glare. The light provided some comfort; experience had taught her that monsters preferred the dark.

Opening her fridge, she removed a carton of orange juice and poured herself a glass. Setting the empty carton aside, she took a long drink. She'd need to brave a trip to the store tomorrow.

In truth, she dreaded her excursions out into the world less lately. She felt . . . safer somehow. Almost at ease. It had been over a year now. A year where she had led a safe, seemingly *human* existence. Fourteen months had passed since her demon attempted a possession. Some days she almost convinced herself that she was a normal woman.

Some nights, eating popcorn in front of her television, or looking for the right kind of shampoo at the grocery store, or brushing her teeth, the awareness of what she was slipped entirely from her consciousness. For those few blessed moments, she felt peace. She forgot that she was a witch who had surrendered her soul to a demon over two thousand years ago.

And then she'd suddenly remember, and the reality would crash down on her.

The repeating nightmares couldn't be coincidental. Was it *his* doing? Balthazar using a new ploy to get at her? Usually he invaded her directly, planting himself inside her mind and taking over her body, but maybe he'd found a new way to torment her.

She squeezed the bridge of her nose. Her head was already starting to ache. Shoving thoughts of Balthazar away, she washed her glass. Putting it back in the cabinet, she moved into her bedroom, determined to return to sleep.

The nightmare probably had nothing to do with Balthazar. Her overactive imagination had probably latched onto some horrible story she'd seen on the news last night.

Climbing into bed, she pulled the warm covers up to her chin and snuggled into them, enjoying her bed. Outside the wind whistled, stirring the wind chimes she'd hung on the porch. It was the longest time she'd stayed in one place. She actually felt comfortable here.

With a deep sigh, she closed her eyes and prayed to a God she was sure no longer heard her prayers that Balthazar continued to stay away. For the first time, she was somewhere that was beginning to feel like home. And even though she didn't deserve it, she didn't want to lose this.

THE FOLLOWING MORNING, TRESA put on her heavy snow boots for the half-mile trek into town. She had an all-terrain vehicle in the garage, but she rarely used it. Maybe the fresh air would help chase away the vestiges of her nightmare. While the nightmare hadn't returned, she'd slept fitfully, as though she feared it would return if she let down her guard.

Standing, she glanced outside. The snow fell swiftly and a shiver coursed down her spine. You'd think after residing in subarctic climes for generations, she'd be used to it.

Shaking her head, she grabbed her thick, hooded parka off the hook and tucked herself into it. Stepping outside, she closed the door and stood on the porch, tugging on her gloves and inhaling the crisp, cold air.

The skin at her nape prickled, and she stilled, gloves half on as her eyes narrowed on the snowy landscape. The bare, snow-packed road stared back at her. Her gaze moved on, scanning the tree line, studying the dark foliage peeking out from the thick blanket of white. She looked for anything, the slightest thing that wasn't part of the natural landscape.

The flesh on her neck still tingled, but she didn't see anything. She usually sensed Balthazar before he made his presence known. Their bond was palpable. If he was here, she'd know.

Of course, there were other things out there. Things like her. Inhuman creatures that had no right to life. Creatures that hunted and preyed on the innocent. That preyed on *her*. Not that she was in any way innocent.

With one last glance to assure herself that no one was lurking about, she set a brisk pace to town, letting the activity warm her blood. Her breath fogged in front of her in froths of white. Her thoughts veered to her nightmare again. The images intruded on her in bursts, like flashes of lightning in the dark.

Soon she was passing the post office that shared space with the police station. It was a small town where everyone knew everyone else. They even knew her. At least what she presented to them: Tresa King, a freelance writer who sometimes, when the courage seized her, volunteered at the nursing home.

When a month had passed and Balthazar hadn't harassed her, she'd thought she'd test the waters and see if socializing attracted his notice and stirred him from wherever he'd gone. She'd chosen solitude not because she wanted to be alone, but because it was the responsible thing to do. No one was safe around her as long as she was under the thumb of a demon.

She'd started out volunteering a few hours a week, reading and visiting with the elderly, ready to flee at the first sign of Balthazar. As the weeks stretched out without sight or sound from him, she took on more hours.

The door of Mountain Pines chimed when

she entered the lobby. She stomped her snowy boots on the heavy rug. The place had that pungent smell found in nursing homes and hospitals, the stench of sickness mingled with antiseptic. The staff took extra care to make the place homey, though, and Tresa always felt comfortable the moment she stepped inside.

The lobby contained several couches and side tables. Lamps emitted a warm, fuzzy glow. There was something comforting about the place.

"Hello, Tresa," Marcie greeted from the desk.

Tresa smiled back, removing her gloves. "Hi. How was your weekend?" Picking up the pen, she scrawled her name on the volunteer clipboard.

"Watched that new Matt Damon movie. Good stuff. Not much else to do . . . Can't believe we got another snowfall this late in the year."

"Yeah." She tugged her scarf down from her lips. "Still steady out there."

Marcie nodded.

Setting down her pen, Tresa flashed her a smile. "I'll have to check out that movie."

Marcie nodded. "Definitely."

Tresa walked the familiar path to the community room. Two women and a man in a bright red vest sat around one of the round tables near the television, staring vaguely at a morning talk show where two women bantered cheerfully and discussed the latest spring fashions.

Tresa stopped at the table and cleared her throat until she snared their attention. Pulling a deck of cards from her pocket, she asked, "Who's up for a game?"

The old man in the vest grinned, revealing a set of perfect dentures. "About time you got here."

THREE

Darius blew his breath into his hands as he leaned against a pole outside the town's lone diner. The aroma of freshly baked bread wafted to his nose, enticing him. It wasn't the only enticement. More than once, the waitress had sent him a tentative smile through the front window as she wiped down tables.

He considered her for a moment and then stared back across the street. It was warmer inside the diner, but his view would be obstructed. And he'd endured far worse things than cold weather.

The wide double doors of Mountain Pines remained shut, sealing *her* in. His heart squeezed tightly in his chest. To have come so far . . . to be this close . . .

It took everything inside him not to rush across the street and barrel through those doors. But there were people in there. He couldn't risk it. He'd have to wait until she was alone. He should have snatched her this morning before she came into town, but when he'd seen her on that front porch, he'd been startled at the sight of her.

He had watched her, sliding on her gloves in such an ordinary manner. Only she wasn't ordinary. She was hell incarnate. He'd always had a basic description of her, and yet the reality of her felt like a punch in the gut.

He didn't know what he'd expected to see, but not the dark-haired willowy female who looked like some woodland fairy. He supposed he expected a demon witch to look more intimidating, more like . . . a witch. *Not so beautiful.*

Disgust curled through him. He'd encountered many beautiful women over his lifetime. This one would not affect him.

He continued to stare at the doors to the nursing home, perplexed at what she was doing in there. Dropping his hands, he burrowed them deep into his pockets. Even with his elevated body temperature, it was damn cold.

The waitress stuck her head out, rubbing her arms against the chill. "Can I help you?"

He offered her a disarming smile. "I'm fine, thank you. Just waiting for someone." He let the power of his stare charm her, blind her to his actual words. Another gift of his curse.

"Okay." She smiled at him rather dazedly.

"Got some sweet buns in the oven. Best around. Sure you wouldn't like to try one?" The vague, besotted look in her eyes suggested she was offering him more than a sweet bun.

But that was the power of his curse. Lycans had no difficulty in luring prey. She wasn't in full control of herself.

"That's tempting. Maybe later."

With a regretful nod, she ducked back inside.

Turning around, he settled his gaze on the squat building just as a snowplow crawled down the middle of the street. The driver sent him a friendly wave. He waved back, trying to be inconspicuous.

Smoke puffed from the nursing home's dual chimneys and he wondered again what nefarious activities she could be up to in there. It couldn't be good, that was for certain. Despite her deceptive exterior, nothing that ever came from Tresa could be good.

He was the proof of that.

"FULL HOUSE." TRESA LAID down her cards with relish. The two ladies groaned and tossed down their cards.

Albert puffed up his chest and displayed his cards. "Four ladies."

Tresa gasped with mock horror. "You're killing me, Al."

The old man cackled, "Pay up."

Glancing around to make sure none of the staff was watching, Tresa dipped into her pocket and pulled out a box of Milk Duds. "Now, don't choke on these, Al. It's bad enough they're hell on your dentures. I don't want to go to your funeral. I look terrible in black."

Albert's sloped shoulders hunched as he laughed in glee.

Pearl batted her hand at Tresa. "I doubt you look terrible in anything, honey."

"Young girls are always beautiful," Al declared. "It's the benefit of youth. Impossible to be anything but attractive."

His two companions nodded sagely, their heads angled in reflection, as though they were recalling the beauty they'd once possessed.

Tresa felt a pang of regret as she looked at them. She was older than all of them by a couple of thousand years. She had no right to be here, walking this earth, but she was. Because of one foolish act, a hastily made bargain that continued to punish her.

Staring at the elderly trio, she accepted that she'd give anything for what they had. Mortality. A soul.

The chime for lunch rang. The room would be crowded soon with those who could still walk unassisted and didn't take meals in their bedrooms.

She slid her cards into the case and stood. "I'll be back. And next time I'll win."

"You say that every time," Pearl teased.

Tresa wagged a playful finger. "One of these days."

"Keep dreaming, doll. Maybe one day it will happen." Al patted his vest where he'd secured his Milk Duds.

Slipping on her coat, she waved good-bye and left.

If possible, it was even colder outside. Snow fell in sheets that cut like razors as she headed toward the small general store. Once inside, she grabbed a handbasket near the door and waved to Mr. Clarke, the owner. She bought only a few items at a time, so he was used to the sight of her.

"Got in some of that sweet corn you like so much," he called.

"Thanks, Mr. Clarke."

She immediately went to the part of the store where she could find her favorite junk food. Pringles, Ding Dongs and a package of those powder-frosted doughnuts. Next came the produce section. She picked out a few corn-cobs to roast in the oven tonight. As she was examining the avocados for any hopefuls, her nape prickled with awareness again.

Swallowing against the sudden dryness in her mouth, she whirled around and peered through the wide window stretching in front of the produce department. Only three cars sat in the parking lot. Her gaze narrowed. No unusual shadows as far as she could tell. A figure walked along the sidewalk across the street, but he was headed in the other direction, toward the hardware store.

Shaking her head, she turned back around and snatched up a too-ripe avocado. Feeling a sense of urgency, she rushed through the rest of her shopping and paid for her items. If Baltha-zar was out there, ready to pounce, it would be better if she was in the privacy of her own home. Better to wrestle for control of herself there, rather than out in the open where some-one might get hurt.

She carefully eyed her surroundings as she left town, her legs eating up the snow-packed ground as she scanned the press of trees at the edge of the road. Nothing stirred save the swaying branches and leaves weighed down by snow.

Gradually the itch in her skin faded. Still, she remained vigilant as she entered her house, bolting the door and closing all the curtains. She drew a deep breath and stood in the center of her small living room, chafing her perspiring palms against her thighs. Tense. Waiting. Half expecting a shadow to leap out at her from the walls.

Several deep breaths later, she finally moved. Balthazar would come when he wanted and there was little she could do about it. Flipping on the television, she welcomed the noise, the distraction, as she unpacked her groceries. She listened to the world news report with only half an ear as she went about shucking and cleaning the corn.

She was pouring herself a drink when the anchorwoman's voice penetrated her consciousness. She turned slowly, a sick churning starting in her belly as she gazed at the well-coiffed blonde with inflated lips staring grimly out of the flat screen.

"With the body count at three, the San Vista Police Department has confirmed that this is the work of a serial killer. The FBI is now on-site, helping local officials with what the residents of San Vista have dubbed the Rose Petal Killer because he surrounds his victims in rose petals . . ."

The glass slipped from Tresa's fingers and crashed at her feet as her nightmare flashed through her mind . . . the rose petals spread lovingly, with a killer's hand.

She'd *seen* that. *Been* there. In the killer's head. It was no coincidence. There was a serial killer out there, and she was witnessing his crimes, living them vicariously through him.

No. Not him. It wasn't a man, she suddenly realized. *She. Her. They weren't dreams at all.*

It was Balthazar's doing.

He'd taken possession of another witch. That explained why he had suddenly become so disinterested in her. He had someone else to vicariously live through, someone else to do his bidding. Someone more willing to commit atrocities.

The police had no idea these killings were being perpetrated by a woman. And not just any woman. A woman with powerful magic at her disposal. The odds of them catching her, stopping her, were slim.

Tresa tore her gaze away from the television and hurried into the small nook off the living room where her computer desk sat. Hands shaking, she logged on, determined to learn everything she could about the Rose Petal Killer.

Before she left for San Vista, she needed to know what she was up against.

She packed only enough clothes for a week. If she stayed longer than that, she could buy more or wash what she had. Hopefully she could take care of this quickly, though. Point the police in the right direction so they could make an arrest.

She stuffed her toiletries into a small bag, her movements clumsy in her haste. The names of the victims floated through her mind. Taylor, Hannah, Shannan. All murdered at the hands of this Rose Petal Killer. She'd seen their photos online. Their faces, so shining and bright, flashed through her mind and made her stomach churn. A sudden draft of cold air slid over her and for a moment, it didn't register. She was accustomed to the cold.

But then she straightened, her hands falling away from her bag.

A familiar energy hummed at her core, the call of her magic, ready to be used. An instinctive defense, one she hadn't felt in a long time. Hadn't needed in a long time.

Her gift was what gave her away; it was like a homing device within her. It was how Balthazar had found her in the first place and how he kept track of her still.

The energy inside her stirred, ready for what her instincts had been warning her about all day. Sucking in a deep breath, she whirled around, almost expecting someone to be standing there—or some*thing*. She released her breath in a shudder. No one. Nothing.

She moved cautiously from her bedroom and stepped inside the living room. The front door stood open, explaining the cold draft. Her gaze flicked around the room.

Seeing nothing, she approached the door with hesitant steps, certain she had locked it. Ignoring the cold bite of wind, she grasped the edge of the door, peering behind it and then stepping out onto the porch, her body tense and alert as she scanned the snow-draped landscape. Nothing. Calling herself all kinds of crazy, she stepped back inside.

That's when the dark shape materialized, moving so quickly she couldn't even make out a face. Just a blur.

The large shape filled her world, came at her in a growling rush. Hard hands closed over her arms, lifting her off her feet.

She struggled, resisting, fighting, punching. Her efforts made no impact. Her fists bounced off hard muscle. Instinct took over. Desperate, she reached deep inside herself and seized hold of the powers she'd long avoided.

Her gaze flicked around the room, propelling objects with the merest glance. Books and vases flew off shelves, striking him. It took only a look, the slightest whisper through her mind, and it was done. Unlike two thousand years ago, she knew how to summon her powers. Under Balthazar's possession, she'd honed her gift.

She aimed a clock at his head. He ducked it.

When he straightened, she paused, assessing him.

He looked her up and down with a face carved from stone. His lip curled in a sneer. "Is that all you've got, witch?"

So he knew what she was.

She let a vase fly, crashing it into his head and shattering the glass into a thousand pieces. He didn't so much as flinch. And then she knew. Her stomach clenched. She was dealing with someone otherworldly.

He moved faster than she could process and seized both her wrists in a single hand. She hid her wince. Just the slightest bit tighter and he could snap her bones.

The list of otherworldly creatures was relatively short. This wasn't a movie with sexy vampires bent on seduction. He could be a slayer, protecting white witches and hunting the demons that hunted them. But that didn't explain what he was doing here. She was a demon witch—a lost cause as far as any slayer was concerned.

So that left two things. He was either a lycan or a dovenatu, a hybrid lycan.

Lifting her chin, she endured his hold. No sense in fighting until she knew for sure what he was.

"What do you want?" she asked with a calm she didn't feel.

His eyes seared her. Her breath caught, froze inside her lungs. His pewter gaze was as cold as the world outside. Just the sight of him, the evidence of his existence, made her stomach churn.

After a long moment, he slid his hands from where they clutched her wrists like iron manacles. She fluttered her fingers, letting the blood rush back. Rubbing out the imprints of his fingers on her flesh, she took a careful step back.

Everything inside her sank and withered. He was a lycan. The first lycan had bred and infected thousands of people. Had killed and destroyed countless more. The creature before her was the legacy of that first lycan.

Her legacy. A result of her careless actions.

She'd successfully cursed Etienne Marshan into *this*. A beast. Balthazar had tricked her. He had failed to explain *how* he intended to curse the man who'd murdered her family.

She scanned the six-foot-plus creature in front of her. His existence, the existence of every lycan, was her fault. There was no penance for that, no way to run from the guilt. To undo all the death, all the misery.

She couldn't even kill herself. Decapitation was the only way to kill a demon witch, and that would free the demon. Her death would grant Balthazar the power to manifest on earth, to walk among man. Then he could wreak even more havoc.

She was the one responsible for creating the monster she now faced. Whatever he did to her, she deserved it. Except she couldn't let him kill her. She couldn't give Balthazar the freedom he'd been craving these many years. Her only reason to live was to thwart him, and to save as many people as she could from him. So this lycan didn't get to kill her. She couldn't let him.

She lifted her chin as she gazed at him. "What do you want?" she repeated coldly, her tone indicating none of the desperation humming through her. With a breath, she let him know she knew what he was. "Lycan."

FOUR

She wasn't what he'd expected.

Up close, he was caught even more off guard at the sight of her. Not that he'd expected her to look like a two-thousand-year-old hag. He didn't look anywhere near his thousand-odd years.

He inhaled thinly through his nose. Her beauty didn't faze him, though. He knew what she was. All she had done. If not for her, he would have lived and died a peaceful existence long ago, his soul intact. And countless lives would have been spared.

"What do I want?" he repeated. "What I want is *you* dead." He raked her with a scathing glare. "Your corpse at my feet. Only that will satisfy me."

She didn't so much as flinch.

He continued, "But I've been told you can't die."

"You're not totally ignorant, then?" She

cocked her head as though in approval. Her glossy dark hair swayed, as smooth as glass around her. "Yes. My death would be a bad idea," she agreed.

He bristled at her condescension. "Unleashing an evil worse than you isn't what I'm after."

She arched an elegant eyebrow. "If you know killing me would release the demon, then why are you here?"

"Because you're the key," he bit out.

She looked bewildered. Again, not the reaction he was expecting from evil incarnate.

Where was the rage? The cruelty?

She shook her head. "The key to what?"

"You started all this." He motioned to himself, and then stilled when he saw that his hand shook ever so slightly. "You have to be able to end it."

Understanding filled her whiskey gold eyes . . . and something else, something he couldn't identify. "You think I can help you?" She considered him slowly, crossing her slim arms in front of her. "What is it you want exactly, lycan?"

The word grated on his nerves—probably because she was to blame for it. That she would sneer the word at him when *she* was the one who had created all lycans . . .

Hostility pumped through his veins. He closed and opened his hands at his sides, fighting the urge to lash out at her for everything she was—everything she had done. Everything she had made him do.

He had hurt people. More than he could ever remember. At moonrise, when he was lost to the lycan curse, no one was safe from him. No man, no woman or child. He could deny none of the atrocities he had committed.

And he wanted to destroy the beast within him. He might have lost his soul, but he believed there was a way to regain his humanity. To rid himself of the moon's curse and live out his life as a normal man might.

"I want you to reverse the curse," he demanded.

She blinked, the pale skin of her smooth forehead creasing in confusion.

"I don't want to be this." He hit his chest, hard. His rage spilled over. "It was never my choice."

She studied him for a long time, her eyes wide with astonishment. She finally understood that he was different. That he didn't want to be a monster.

"You're not like the others . . ." Her voice

faded. She might understand, but she was still clearly confused.

He nodded. "That's right. I'm not." He was a lycan looking for redemption. Such a thing wouldn't make sense to her. He could hardly fathom it himself.

Her body language eased a bit. Tossing back her head, she laughed. The sound was low and throaty, but lacking all humor.

It was the last thing he could handle. Especially from *her*. His hand lashed out to seize her throat.

Her laughter died. Her eyes fixed on his face. He drew her closer. "What's so amusing, witch?"

"I would love to reverse the curse. I'm laughing because you think it can be done. That I can do it."

"You had the magic to create us."

"It was the demon's power. Not mine."

He shook his head, swallowing a growl. "There has to be a way to . . ." His voice faded as he searched for words.

"There has to be a way to *uncreate* you?" she finished, clawing at his hand on her neck. "It doesn't work that way."

"How does it work?"

"Let me go."

He didn't budge.

Her fiery gaze clashed with his. "Let. Me. Go."

Time stretched between them as he gazed into her mesmerizing eyes, and he couldn't help wondering if she was working some of her magic on him now, because he couldn't look away.

At last he slid his hand from the soft skin of her throat and took a step back. "Aren't your eyes supposed to be black?" he muttered. It was something he'd run across consistently in his research about demon witches.

"My demon's not home right now," she explained grimly, lightly touching her throat.

"Your demon can come and go?" He frowned. Did that mean that she could reverse the curse only when she was possessed?

"Yes. He hasn't bothered me in over a year."

Bothered her? As though he were a nuisance.

"And I hope it stays that way," she added.

She regretted entering into a contract with the demon? He shook his head. Whether she regretted her choices didn't change anything. "How can you get him to come back?"

"You don't want him here."

"No, *you* don't. I do."

"You think he's just going to listen to you

and end the curse?" She shook her head. The motion struck him somehow as tired. "It's not that easy. Dealing with him . . . you *can't* deal with him. Trust me."

"Let me decide—"

"You don't know what you're dealing with. He won't help you. The first thing he did upon possessing me was curse Etienne Marshan. I don't even remember that happening." A muscle flickered in the delicate line of her jaw. "When I'm under his influence, I can barely remember my actions . . . everything is a hazy dream, at best."

She turned her back on him and moved into the living area, her movements relaxed. Without fear. That was a change. Once females knew what he was, they tended to scream and run. Except for Helen, of course. He couldn't get rid of her if he wanted to.

He watched as she sat on the couch, her pale, elegant hands clasping her knees. He'd never seen a woman move with such easy grace . . . and then he reminded himself that she wasn't a woman. She was an abomination. Just like him. Her every move was probably calculated to manipulate, to drag weak men into her web. Lucky for him he was neither weak nor man.

Her cat eyes reached deep inside him, assessing. Again, he wondered if she was attempting some spell to charm him.

"I can't help you," she said evenly, moistening her lips as if she was nervous. "I'm sorry. I appreciate that you aren't like other lycans and—"

"I don't give a damn what you appreciate," he snapped. "You're the reason I'm this." He grabbed two handfuls of his shirtfront roughly.

She maintained her composure and drew a deep breath. "I wish I could help you, but I can't."

He eyed her dubiously. She actually sounded sorry, but he knew that couldn't be true.

"If I could take it back . . ." She glanced away for a moment before looking back to him. Almost as though her composure was slipping.

He sank down on the chair across from her, every muscle still taut and braced for attack, even as unlikely as an attack seemed from this slight female with a deceptively vulnerable air. She was quite the little actress. But then, she'd had years to perfect her act. Right now she was meek. Polite. But it didn't fool him. Her witch soul was even uglier than his. "I'm supposed to believe you? Accept your apology and walk away?"

She rolled one shoulder in a small shrug. "What else is there for you to do? I can't help you."

"I think with the right incentive . . . you just might figure out a way to give me what I want."

Her eyes flared as the words hung between them, laden with threat. The air thickened between them. His gaze narrowed in on the rapidly thumping pulse at her throat, studying it intently above her collar.

She settled her hands on her lap carefully. For a moment he thought they trembled, but then he decided that wasn't possible. Not her. She'd have to feel something to be affected like that, and he knew she was as cold-blooded as they came.

"I can't tell you what I don't know. If there is a way to end the curse, I don't know how to do it. Balthazar would hardly confide that to me." She rose to her feet, standing rigidly, stretching her five and a half feet. "Now. I was just packing."

He rose to his feet. She really thought she could dismiss him. She thought she was safe from him because he couldn't kill her. Well, there were plenty of other unpleasant things he could do to her.

He appraised her coolly. "Where are you going?"

"Anchorage."

He cocked his head, convinced that wasn't the entire truth. "Anchorage is south of here. I've been tracking you for a while now. Through Canada, Alaska. You never go south. Especially in spring."

She fidgeted. "Yeah, well. I thought it was time for a change of scenery."

She was lying. He smelled it on her.

She moved to the front door, stepping over the broken objects littering the carpet, motioning for him to follow.

Her face was stoic, but the wariness was still in her eyes. In her unwillingness to look him directly in the face. She was hiding something. Maybe she really knew how to end the curse and was keeping it from him. She pulled open the door, letting in a burst of frigid air.

He reached beyond her and grasped the door, wrapping his fingers around the edge.

She flinched at the abrupt move, his sudden closeness, and looked up at him, uncertainty bright in her eyes.

He shut the door solidly, the resounding click gratifying. Flattening his palms against its surface, he caged her in with his arms. "I'm not going anywhere. And neither are you."

*   *   *

TRESA JIGGLED THE HANDCUFF at her wrist that chained her to the side of the headboard. Flipping her legs around, she planted her feet flat on the floor so that she was in a sitting position.

She scanned the room, identifying objects she might be able to use to help her escape. If she concentrated, she could probably break the bedpost she was cuffed to. Then she exhaled in frustration. She'd used her powers earlier when the lycan first showed up, and Balthazar had undoubtedly sensed her. Any more uncharacteristic activity from her and he might decide to pay her a visit. The last thing she needed was Balthazar around while she tried to defuse this lycan hell-bent on destroying him.

Glaring at the open door of her bedroom, she shouted, "This isn't necessary!"

A moment passed before he emerged, propping his broad shoulder against the doorjamb. All six feet plus of him. Her chest tightened at the sight of him. Physically, he was an impressive specimen. She had thought her little house spacious, but with him in it, it felt crowded. Overwhelmed.

His piercing pewter eyes, set deeply beneath a slash of dark brows, absorbed her. She couldn't escape their singe.

"Did you say something?" He possessed a faint accent . . . something that had faded from what it once was, but it was there nonetheless. She recognized it as something obsolete, the echo of a world long gone.

She glowered at him. "You heard me." Along with all her other shouts since he'd hauled her from the living room and handcuffed her to the bed. *Damn.* No way would she make it to Anchorage now in time for her flight.

Her gaze narrowed. In the last half hour, she'd heard him moving around her house and the telltale beeps of the computer starting up. Clearly, he was nosing through her stuff.

"This isn't necessary," she repeated, her voice even but tight.

He cocked his head. "Give me the answers I need and we can end this." He looked her over, his cold eyes contemptuous. She resisted a shiver. It had been a long time since someone looked at her with that kind of hatred. She lived her life anonymously. No one knew what she was, what she had done. Maybe the only blessing of her life.

But from him she could not hide.

"I can't destroy you." He nodded his head once. "I accept that." He pushed off the doorjamb and moved into the room, stopping directly in front of her. "But the solution is you. It's *in* you. Whether you know it or not."

She inhaled a deep breath. He was beyond persuading, and most important—most frightening—he wasn't going to leave anytime soon. She looked around her room helplessly. "What do you suggest we do?"

Towering over her, he crossed his arms. "We need your demon."

She sucked in a deep breath and shook her head doggedly. "I can't summon him."

I won't.

He drilled her with his gaze, his look grim, his square jaw hard and unyielding. Clearly he wasn't buying it.

She moistened her lips and amended this by adding, "I don't know if I can." Balthazar had a new witch to play with. Apparently one more willing to participate in his evil games than Tresa was. Even if she tried to summon him, he probably wouldn't come.

He shrugged as if he had all the time in the world. "Then we're going to be here awhile, I guess." He turned and walked away, his steps thudding across the floor.

Furious heat flamed her face. She clamped her lips shut and screamed inside, only a muffled screech escaping. She yanked at her arm, pulling at the handcuff encircling her wrist, heedless of the pain.

His chuckle carried from the living room. He was enjoying tormenting her. Of course— he hated her.

After several moments of useless struggle, she fell back on the bed with a huffed breath and gazed up at the ceiling. Desperate tears burned her eyes.

This lycan was seriously interfering in her plans. Biting down on her lip, she contemplated telling him the truth. That her demon had found a new plaything who was committing terrible murders, and she needed to stop her. It was just a matter of time before the witch killed again. Balthazar would see to that. And meanwhile, she was stuck here.

In the end, she decided to keep that information to herself. The less the lycan knew what she was thinking, the better. This lycan didn't care about anything except reversing his curse. And she was his prisoner until he figured out that that wasn't ever going to happen.

Helplessness washed over her, and she dropped her head back on the bed and closed her eyes. Tears seeped out, rolling hotly down her cheeks. She brushed at her eyes to wipe the moisture away but the handcuff stopped her, digging into her wrist.

With a choked curse, she rolled onto her side and buried her head in the pillow, damned if she would let him hear her weep.

FIVE

She knew it was tomato-basil soup before he appeared in her room. The savory aroma made her stomach growl. It was her favorite, which was why she had so many jars in her pantry.

He filled the threshold, pausing a moment to settle those silver eyes on her. She scooted as far back against the headboard as she could.

He moved into the room and set the tray on the bed, near her legs. "Thought you might be hungry."

"I'm not." Her stomach rumbled in denial.

He motioned to her food. "You'll need your strength."

"For what?" she snapped.

"Contacting your demon."

She laughed mirthlessly. "You watch too much TV. It's not like contacting the dead. I'm not a medium."

"Then how do you do it?" There was an edge of desperation to his voice. He wanted this.

Badly. It was why he had come. What would he do to her when he couldn't get his way?

"It's up to Balthazar," she said. "I can't summon him."

The flesh of his jaw pulled tight. Clearly this wasn't the answer he wanted. "Then we wait."

Her pulse spiked and she sat up straighter. "For how long?"

"However long it takes. He won't ignore you forever." His gaze skimmed over her then. It was an assessing look, coldly admiring. "We have plenty of time on our hands."

"What about the full moon?" she challenged. "How do you expect to stay here and not attack me?"

He moved away from the bed. "Clearly, we'll have to relocate in a few weeks to someplace more secure."

Leave? With him? And go where? She shook her head. She didn't even know his name. At the sudden thought, she asked, "What's your name?" When he simply stared at her as though he wouldn't confide that much, she flung out, "Come on. You know mine."

After a stretch of silence, he answered, "Darius."

Darius. An old name. Although he couldn't be older than she was, she knew she faced someone nearly as ancient. He would not be easy to escape—even with her gifts. And she didn't want to use her powers. Didn't want to lure Balthazar back in. Nothing, not even this lycan, would change her mind about that.

"I'm not going anywhere with you, Darius."

At the door, he stopped and looked over his shoulder at her. A faintly sinister smile curled his lips. "You think you have a choice?"

An angry epithet rose to her lips. He was wrong if he thought she was some helpless female to be kept in chains indefinitely.

She shook her head at him slowly. "You have no idea what I'm capable of."

His pewter eyes iced over, chilling her to the core. "Oh, I know exactly what you're capable of . . . *witch*."

She flinched at the cruel emphasis he placed on the last word.

Without saying anything else, he turned and left the room. She stared at the empty door for a long moment, fighting back the urge to shout after him that she wasn't this horrible being he thought her. *She wasn't . . .*

The words stuck in her throat. She'd have to fully believe that to say it.

*   *   *

DARIUS STOOD SILENTLY BESIDE the bed, looking down, watching the witch sleep. He crossed his arms. He'd found her. The demon witch he'd hunted since he stumbled upon the knowledge of her existence three years ago. It was best to think of her in those terms. *Demon witch*. Not Tresa. Not female. Not woman.

Her chest rose and fell evenly. The tears hadn't yet dried on her cheeks and an uncomfortable knot formed in his chest.

The demon witch he had envisioned in his head, the one responsible for creating the first lycan that had gone on to spawn thousands, wasn't supposed to weep.

He cocked his head as he looked down at her. She was all too human. At least she appeared that way. He cursed softly beneath his breath and shook his head. She was an evil, soul-sucking witch. He was a fool to consider her anything less.

He walked back into the living room, fired up his computer and opened one of many research files, reviewing everything he had on demons. If she was right, he would need to deal directly with this Balthazar.

His phone rang. A glance down confirmed it was Helen.

He answered. "Hello, Helen."

"Darius, where are you?" In addition to being his housekeeper, Helen liked to play the role of mother. Forget that he was a thousand years older than her fifty-something. He blamed it on the fact that she had stayed with him all these years, wasting her life to serve him. He had encouraged her to leave and build a life of her own, but Helen couldn't be told to do anything she didn't want to.

"Alaska."

Silence greeted him on the other end. He could read her silence perfectly. She wasn't happy.

"You're still looking for her," she finally declared.

"Actually"—he glanced over his shoulder as if he could see through the wall into her bedroom—"I've found her."

"You found her?" Excitement laced her voice. "And did she do it? Did you make her—?

"She doesn't know how."

Another pause, and then a breathy, "Oh." The heavy word said it all.

Helen knew what he was. He'd saved her from a lycan attack years ago, and he hadn't been able to shake her ever since. She claimed she owed him her life.

"So you're coming home?" she asked.

"Not yet."

"Not yet?" The anxiousness returned to her voice. "But you need to—"

"I still have time. It's a couple more weeks until moonrise."

"But what reason do you have for staying? She's useless to you."

"She claimed she doesn't know how to reverse the curse, but I still think she's the answer."

"Darius," she sighed his name, sounding tired, and he was reminded that she was getting older. "What are you doing?" Weariness weighed on her words, making him feel like he was a fool on same insane crusade.

"Look, I have to go, Helen. It's complicated. I'll be home before moonrise."

She was still talking when he hung up the phone. He waited a moment to see if she would call again. When she didn't, he leaned back in his chair and rubbed the bridge of his nose. His eyes ached. He couldn't remember the last time he'd had a good night's sleep.

He cared about Helen, but she couldn't understand his need, his desperation to . . . *fix* himself. To kill the part of him that was monstrous and evil, intent only on destroying life.

Helen didn't understand what he had been.

She didn't know the truth about the night he saved her. That he had been tempted to join the lycans attacking her and tear her apart.

He fought the monster living inside him every day. Not just at moonrise. She thought he was good, but he was lost. As lost as that witch in the next room.

DARIUS WASN'T SURE WHAT woke him. He blinked and sat up, board straight, in the chair where he'd fallen asleep, an ancient text of demonology in his lap. Every nerve was stretched taut and vibrated with alertness.

With silent movements, he set the book on the table and moved through the house, the glow from the living room lamp lighting his way. He checked first on Tresa.

She slept on, her hair a splash of ink against the white pillowcase. She looked vulnerable, her features soft and relaxed in sleep. Something unfurled inside his chest at the sight. He snapped his thoughts free with a single hard shake of his head.

The tray of food he'd brought her sat on the floor, her dinner eaten.

Satisfied that she wasn't the reason he'd woken, he moved from her room and surveyed the main living area. It was dark out. Black seeped through the curtains of the wide front window. Silenced throbbed all around him. The kind of silence that made someone feel like they were the only person left on earth.

He walked to the door, his footsteps a dull thud against the wood floor. He unlocked the door and stepped out onto the porch. The cold hung thick and swirling on the opaque air. He squinted, looking deep into the snow-draped horizon. The winds stirred, a distant rush on the night. Nothing moved on the ground or in the trees.

He turned to move back inside, but then stopped, inhaling deeply. And that's when he caught the loathsome odor, sweetly bitter and acrid.

Silver.

He whirled around just as a bullet whistled toward him. He jerked aside as it plugged the outside wall of the house.

Then they were everywhere.

They streamed from the trees. A small army, maybe twenty. Black camo, night-vision goggles secured to their faces, weapons at the ready. They charged for the house, shouting directions at one another.

He dove back inside and slammed the door

shut, seizing the moment it gave him to ready himself. He centered himself in the middle of the room, bracing for the onslaught.

The door crashed open and they swarmed inside, shouting. He faced them. This is how they destroyed his kind, he thought grimly. Using sheer volume to overpower, to beat down and conquer beasts bred to kill.

His muscles bunched tight as the intruders circled him. He waited for the worst. He imagined they would slam him with silver bullets, but they didn't.

The shot never came, never tore through his flesh.

One hunter stepped ahead of the others and stopped directly in front of Darius. He pulled his night goggles off and smiled humorlessly. "Thought you were rid of me, didn't you, bastard?"

Darius recognized him at once. "Sam," he murmured. "Good to see you."

"You remembered my name? I'm flattered." Sam lifted his rifle higher, aiming squarely for Darius's chest.

Before Sam could squeeze off a shot, Darius wrenched the weapon free, snapping it in his grip.

A bullet ripped into his chest. He jerked

from the force, hissing in pain. Another rifle was jabbed into his face. "Easy there. Settle down. The bullet inside you isn't silver, but this one is."

He growled low in his throat, but said nothing. He was lucky he was alive. Even as he stood, panting in pain, he could feel his body rejecting the bullet, pushing it free from his shredded muscle and sinew.

One of the other hunters burst into their midst. "You gotta see this!" He motioned excitedly toward the bedroom. "The animal's got a woman handcuffed to a bed."

Sam's lip curled at him. "Sick fuck. You like torturing innocent women? Well, we're going to have fun with you. See how you like it." That said, he pulled the trigger.

Darius jerked at the second bullet to tear through him. Instead of the burn of silver, he felt only more discomfort. He swallowed a cry. Nothing he couldn't handle. Nothing that would kill him.

He looked down and spotted the end of a protruding dart in his chest. Not a bullet—a tranq. He seized it and pulled it clean, tossing it to the floor with a grunt.

His gaze drifted back up. The hunters' faces swirled in front of him, blurring until their features became indistinct smudges. The edge of his vision grayed, and then blackened. He dropped, hard, to his knees and swayed.

Sam took advantage and kicked him in the ribs. Once. Twice. He heard the crunch of bone and knew the hunter had cracked his ribs. He fell to the floor, clutching his side. He'd broken bones before. They'd heal. Not that he expected any of these hunters to keep him alive long enough for that. They'd torment him to the end, never giving him a chance to heal. Only giving him a chance to feel and breathe the pain.

The fog rolled in, muddling his thoughts. The blackness grew, spreading until he could see nothing. Feel nothing. Until he was no more.

SIX

The handcuff fell free from her wrist. Tresa sighed with relief and rubbed the tender flesh.

"Thank you," she breathed as the hunter stepped back, giving her space.

Another hunter stood at the door, staring her down as if she were a great nuisance. "You okay?" he asked gruffly. He glanced from her back to the living room, obviously more interested in whatever was going on there.

Darius. She inhaled sharply. *What were they doing to him?*

Several moments passed before the hunter looked back, settling his dark eyes on her expectantly, and she realized she hadn't responded yet.

"You okay?" he repeated.

She nodded jerkily, feeling the overwhelming urge to inquire after Darius and see what they were doing to him. Not exactly what a victim would do, though.

His dark gaze slid over her. "Do you require medical care?"

Obviously they thought Darius had injured her.

"N-no. I'm fine. What about . . . *him*? What are you going to do with him?"

His dark gaze sharpened on her, and she realized she might have sounded concerned. Which was ridiculous. Why should she care what happened to him? His assessment continued, sweeping over her and missing nothing. Not her mussed and tangled hair. Not her wrinkled clothing. The sleeve of her sweater was ripped at the shoulder. God knows what he thought Darius had done to her.

"Don't worry. He'll get what he deserves. We'll see to that." He looked to the other hunter, standing near the bed. "C'mon, Klonsky. Give her a minute alone." He looked back at her. "Miss, we'll be out here. Just take your time."

She nodded as they started to leave. Klonsky's gaze lingered on her, pitying and kind. A look that wouldn't last if he knew what she was.

Once alone, she dropped back on the bed, rubbing the tender skin of her wrist. A heavy sigh escaped her. Male voices drifted from the other room, accompanied by the thud of feet. What was she going to do with a houseful of hunters? What would they do if they figured out she was more than some hapless female who had fallen into the clutches of a ravenous lycan? She gulped, somehow certain her fate would be better in Darius's hands than in theirs. In either case, she wasn't sticking around to put their goodwill to the test.

Rising to her feet, she quickly changed clothes, her movements hurried as nervousness tripped through her. She didn't want one of them to walk in on her half naked. Sucking in a deep breath, she moved for the door, opening it carefully. Almost instantly a hunter was there, blocking her way.

"You need something?" he asked.

"Uh, yeah . . . I want to leave."

"That's not possible at this time."

She blinked at his matter-of-fact response. Moistening her lips, she strove for an even tone. "Look. I appreciate all of you helping me, but I'd really just like to leave you to . . . whatever it is you're doing and get out of here."

He glanced over his shoulder, almost as if checking to see if someone else was going to step in and handle the situation—handle *her*.

She followed his gaze, looking over his

shoulder. She gasped, spotting Darius strapped to a chair, silver chains looped around his body. Tendrils of smoke rose, curling on the air. He was naked from the waist up and unconscious, his head lolling, blessedly oblivious to his roasting body. Steam rose from where the silver seared into his flesh, eating deep into the skin.

Clamps bit into his chest, and her mouth dried. They meant to torture him. Her stomach roiled.

The hunter pushed her back into her room. "We've got our hands full at the moment. We need to be ready when he wakes up." He jerked a thumb behind him to Darius. "Give us some time. We'll figure out what to do with you."

"What to *do* with me?" she echoed. "You don't have to *do* anything with me except let me go."

"It's not that simple. You've seen things today that you don't have any business knowing about." He grasped her shoulder, either to calm her or push her back in the room—she wasn't sure which.

"I assure you I can forget everything that's happened." She knew these hunters prized the secrecy of their existence—not to mention the secrecy of lycans' existence. "I won't talk to anyone. I promise. Who would believe me?"

He patted her shoulder. "Stay put and we'll be with you soon, sweetheart."

Sweetheart. The word rankled. His condescension rankled. She was almost tempted to explain to him just what she was and what she could do. Of course, that would probably be the end of her. Assuming they knew to decapitate her.

Before she could say anything else, he shut the door in her face. She slapped the wall with a frustrated growl. Whirling around, she paced the room, trying to erase the image of Darius strapped in that chair, prepped for all manner of horrible torture. She needed to worry about herself, about stopping Balthazar's new witch. Not about some lycan.

He probably deserved whatever they did for his past deeds. His very existence was a threat, a risk to innocent lives everywhere. She shouldn't care about his fate.

She *shouldn't.*

CONSCIOUSNESS RETURNED GRADUALLY. LIKE an annoying gnat buzzing about his head, Darius tried to push it away, reluctant to embrace it. When pain coursed through his body he gasped, his head shooting straight up, eyes wide and aching as he surveyed his surroundings, instantly assessing his position in the middle of a roomful of hunters.

"He's awake," several of them shouted. They tightened their ranks around him, their anxiousness palpable. They reminded him of children at the circus, eager for the show.

As his awareness sharpened, so did the pain. He struggled against the silver chains restraining him, hissing and going still at the fresh wave of agony. The sweet odor of searing flesh filled his nose. Smoke lifted from him as if he was a piece of meat on the grill.

"Hurts, doesn't it?" Sam asked from beside him, his eyes glittering with satisfaction.

He swallowed back a response, afraid a plea would escape. He'd beg nothing of this hunter. Of any of them. They couldn't hurt him as much as he'd suffered already, countless times in countless lives.

Pushing the pain aside, his thoughts jumped to Tresa. What had they done with her? A quick glance to her bedroom revealed the door to be shut. Was she still cuffed in there? He felt himself leaning forward against his chains. The fire burned hotter in his chest and arms.

"What'd you do with her?" he demanded.

Several hunters exchanged looks and he

immediately regretted the words, realizing he'd come off sounding worried. Letting them think he meant to make a meal out of her put her in a better position. He didn't examine why he should want to protect her. He just did.

"The woman you had cuffed to that bed? She's fine," one of them answered. "Fortunately we got to her before you could ruin her."

Darius curled his lips in a deliberate sneer. "Too bad. She would have tasted sweet."

"Bastard." A fair-haired hunter lunged forward, his face flushed angrily. His comrades pulled him back.

Darius chuckled. "After a few weeks with me, moonrise wouldn't have come soon enough for her. She would have begged me to finish her off."

The young hunter flailed wildly, intent on breaking through his friends to reach Darius. They forced him outside. "Walk it off, Klonsky."

Apparently Tresa had gained a savior. He ignored his flash of annoyance. He should be relieved. He wouldn't put it past these hunters to kill her so she didn't spread word of their existence—or the existence of lycans. It wouldn't be the first time hunters had killed in the name of their cause.

Sam got in his face. "You like brutalizing women, dog?"

Darius chuckled. The man sounded so heroic. "Actually, I don't. Would you believe I abstain from violence and feeding on humans? Every full moon I lock myself away . . ."

Sam snorted and his hand lashed out, grinding deeper the silver chain directly over Darius's heart.

Darius cringed, tensing against the pain, his body going as straight as a charged wire.

"Enough," a voice commanded.

Still glowering down at Darius, Sam stepped back, allowing another hunter to move directly in front of him. He was middle-aged and possessed none of Sam's ferocity as he coolly looked Darius over.

Darius took several deep breaths, staring at this hunter through the steam smoldering off his body. "What do you want with me?" He was no fool. If they hadn't killed him yet, it was because they wanted something.

Clearly this hunter was the group's leader. His features revealed nothing as he assessed Darius. "Intel, of course. You're a very old lycan. You must know a great deal about other packs out there."

"I've been running solo a long time. I *don't* know about others out there."

He motioned to Darius's body with a smooth

wave of his hand. "Your end is inevitable. How much pain you want to suffer first is up to you. Silver is the only thing that can kill you," he reminded Darius unnecessarily. "But let me assure you that my imagination is limitless. Over the years, I've learned that a lycan can withstand a lot of abuse." For a long moment he held Darius's gaze, as though he wanted his point—and the *fear*—to settle in.

Darius let loose a single laugh. "And over the years, I've learned that pain is relative."

A flicker of irritation flared in the hunter's eyes, the first sign of emotion Darius had detected from him. "Indeed. Then let's begin." He nodded to Sam.

With an avid grin, Sam made certain the clamps on Darius's chest were secure. Darius held the leader's gaze, his expression blank as he forced his mind to glide away . . . to drift to a place where he could wait out the onslaught of torture.

Sam stepped away and flipped a switch on a device sitting on the coffee table. Instantly, electricity flooded Darius's body. The force of it arched his spine, driving him to pull against the ropes of silver.

He clenched his teeth, trying to swallow back the scream, but it was useless. He couldn't hold silent against the torture.

SEVEN

The door to her room opened. Tresa scrambled off the bed where she'd been curled up in a ball, trying to block out the sound of Darius's screams. At the first cries, she had trembled and pulled the pillow over her head. But it did no good. She shook at the sound of his screams, imagining the pain he was suffering.

And she'd wept. She couldn't help herself. With his every shout, every low, keening moan, she felt herself splintering inside. The knowledge that she had done this—that she was responsible for *him,* for what he was . . . for the existence of these hunters . . .

It was too much.

Several times she had stood up, determined to rush through the door and try to stop them, the overwhelming need to explain that he wasn't the type of lycan they should be hunting burning on her lips. It wasn't his fault that he was what he was.

She stopped each time, reminding herself that if she showed the slightest sympathy, they'd likely strap her up beside him and inflict the same torture on her. She had to keep silent. Save herself. Escape. Balthazar was out there with his new witch, and their killing spree had to be stopped.

Darius had fallen silent over an hour ago. She'd watched the clock, timing the ominous silence. At least his screams had told her he still lived. Now she could only wonder if he was still alive.

Klonsky smiled uncertainly at her. "You doing better?" he asked, smoothing a hand over his fair, feathery hair.

"Yes. Thank you." She nodded, straining for a glimpse beyond his shoulder.

"Come on." He motioned for her to follow him from the room.

She hesitated, unsure. What did they want with her? Had they decided she was a liability? A witness they couldn't keep alive?

"It's okay," he reassured her. "We decided you can go."

"I can?" She blinked. They were letting her go? She could just stroll out of here?

He moved to grasp her elbow. "I persuaded them to let you go. You can come back after we've left."

As if she would ever return here. "Th-thanks."

He peered down at her, his gaze intense. "Forget what you saw. No one will believe you even if you tell. But if we hear anything, if you show up on some talk show, we'll find you . . ." He let his sentence trail off ominously.

She didn't need him to elaborate. They had tracked down Darius. A feat in itself, she suspected. He didn't seem like the sort to let himself get captured.

She nodded fiercely. "I understand. I won't talk."

"Good girl." Patting her arm in an irritating manner, he led her from the room.

The hunters were all still here. None so much as glanced at her. A few sat at her kitchen table, inspecting their gear. Another peered inside her refrigerator. She clenched her jaw and tried not to look bothered by their total invasion of her home. She just needed to get out of here.

She stumbled when she caught sight of Darius in the center of the room. He was still strapped to the chair, his flesh bloody and raw, exposed where the silver chains looped around him. Bile rose in the back of her throat. His head sagged, and for a moment she thought he was dead. But then his head lifted, slowly, as if the effort pained him.

As though he sensed her, those startling pewter eyes locked on her. Well, at least one eye did. His right eye was badly swollen and sealed shut.

She felt trapped, pinned beneath his stare. It was impossible to look away. His face revealed nothing, no expression, just the ravages of his beatings. A hot stab of pity twisted through her. And guilt, too.

She inhaled a ragged breath. She shouldn't feel guilty that the lycan who'd held her captive was in this predicament. He might deserve her pity, but she shouldn't feel *guilty*. He'd heal. As much as he suffered, as bad as he looked, these weren't mortal wounds.

Her gaze drifted to the pistols the hunters carried, certain no ordinary bullets sat in those chambers. Who was she kidding? It was just a matter of time before they killed him with a silver bullet.

He's not your concern, Tresa.

She squared her shoulders and told herself to forget the lycan. He was not her responsibility. She couldn't save him.

She reached for her bag, trampled and shoved against the wall, still near the door where she'd left it the day before. Had it only been hours? It felt like days as she'd sat in her room listening to Darius's cries. She fought the urge to look back at him again.

Klonsky reached for the handle of her bag. "You sure you'll be okay? I can take you into town."

"Klonksy," another hunter called, his voice annoyed. "Let her go."

"I'm fine," she murmured, reaching to take her bag from him, eager to be free of this testosterone-charged room.

Klonksy ignored the other hunter and dipped his head to meet her gaze. He smiled. Charmingly, she supposed, if her heart weren't pounding a hundred beats a second. Either he was flirting with her or he was sincerely concerned for her welfare. Whatever the case, she didn't care.

He took her arm as if she were something delicate. As if she required escorting. How quickly his treatment of her would alter if he knew what she really was.

She slid her arm free. "I can manage. Thank you."

"You heard her, Klonksy," the other hunter called out again, his blunt features reflecting his impatience. "Leave her be and get back to the job."

She swallowed against the thickness in her

throat. *The job.* The job of exterminating lycans. Mostly a good thing, except this one, Darius . . . he was different. She knew that.

Picking up her bag, she moved for the door. All the while, she imagined she felt Darius's gaze burning on her back from where he sat. A prisoner. Awaiting his execution.

DARIUS TORE HIS GAZE off the door through which Tresa had just departed. With his one good eye, he'd observed her clearly as she strolled out of the house, out of his grasp, without a backward glance.

The hunter Sam stared after her with a dazed expression. Taken in by a witch. He supposed he could understand that. She'd affected him, too. She'd made him question his conviction that she was every bit as bad as her demon.

It was tempting to forget what she was, what she had done. Lucky for him, he was practiced at denying himself temptation.

Tearing his gaze from the door, he commanded himself to forget her. He needed to focus on survival. He'd hunt her down again later.

The pain from the silver was a constant now. Unremitting. A deep burning in his flesh.

A sting that radiated through his body. If he moved, fresh agony would stab him, fresh smoke would waft from him. He inhaled thinly through his nostrils and let his head droop and loll. Best if they thought him weak and beaten.

He surveyed them from beneath his lashes, taking a head count. Eighteen hunters armed to the teeth. Tough odds. One fatal shot from a silver bullet and he was finished. Not that he had anything to lose. He'd be dead if he stayed, if he didn't try to escape.

He held himself motionless, readying for his next move, waiting for the right moment.

Tresa tried not to run once she stepped outside the house, certain that would only draw suspicion. But then, she supposed a woman suffering abduction and abuse at the hands of a lycan might run. That thought in her mind, she didn't worry when her steps quickened.

She fumbled with the garage opener in her bag and opened the door behind which her SUV sat parked. Still shaking, she didn't wait to let the engine warm up. She backed out and gunned it down the driveway to the road, glancing several times in the rearview mirror, almost expecting to see Darius giving chase behind her. Ridiculous, of course. He wasn't going anywhere.

He wasn't going anywhere ever again.

Her stomach twisted sickly and she struck the steering wheel with her fist.

They wouldn't kill him swiftly. She'd seen that in their eyes. They reminded her of other men, from a long time ago. Knights who'd invaded her home with the same mercilessness in their eyes. Heartless assassins, they carried the same stink, eager to follow commands to destroy and take life.

A shiver scraped her spine. She shook it off and focused on the road, telling herself that one less lycan on earth was a good thing. Even if he *was* actually searching for his soul . . . searching for redemption.

Just like you are. Like you've always done.

Damnit. She hit the steering wheel again, suddenly feeling worse. He *wasn't* like her. He wished her dead. If he could get away with killing her, he would have. And he would have enjoyed it. And yet even in those cursed pewter eyes, something else had glowed. Something that resembled humanity. More humanity than she had witnessed in the hunters.

With a curse, she slammed on the brakes. The car skidded on the road, spraying snow up onto her windshield. Panting as though she'd run a marathon, she stared out at the vast whiteness.

After several deep breaths, she put the car in reverse and backed around in a small circle, the engine revving. Once turned fully, she drove back toward her house, stopping just before she'd be visible to those inside.

Leaving the car running, she stepped out into the biting cold, weaving like a wraith between trees until she could see the house. Biting her lip, she considered her options. Darius was strong, even if he wasn't in full manifest. He could break free if the odds were only slightly more in his favor. He just needed a little help. Just a nudge from her . . .

She scanned the snowdrifts surrounding the house, looking for something, anything. If she could create a diversion, it would shake the hunters up a bit. Maybe Darius could take advantage of the moment and make his escape.

He'd have a chance. It was all she could give him. All she could attempt. Anything more and she risked not escaping to stop Balthazar's new witch. If Darius couldn't escape, then, well . . . she could do nothing more for him.

Praying that Balthazar was too preoccupied with his new witch, that it was too cold here for him, that she was just too big a pain in the ass for him, she surrendered to her magic.

She focused her attention on a tall pine tree several yards from her kitchen window, concentrating until her head ached and she began to shake, her limbs trembling.

Satisfaction curled through her as the leaves began to shudder, snow falling from them in fat clumps of white. Pinecones dropped like nuts from the branches. Her satisfaction grew, as did the throbbing inside her head. She pushed through it, fought it, and delved deep to where the energy hummed within her core.

Wood cracked and snapped. Her entire body was shaking now, the blood pounding painfully in her veins, but she didn't stop, didn't lessen her focus. The tree started to sway as if undecided. She focused harder, straining, pushing her will. *Snap!*

As though a giant hand swooped down and gave it a mighty push, the tree fell hard, directly onto her house.

She couldn't have aimed any better. The garage and right side of her house were crushed beneath a thousand pounds of tree.

She knew Darius was in the living room, free from the worst of the damage. Even from where she stood, her fingers digging into the trunk of a nearby tree, she could hear the shouts of men from inside. Her pulse raced, a wild tempo against her neck. Her eyes ached, trying to glimpse Darius in all that rubble, even as unlikely as that was. Her ears strained, trying to make out the shouted words. Shaking her head, she forced herself to turn away.

If Darius didn't take advantage of the sudden life vest she'd tossed him, then he mustn't want to live that badly.

With an abrupt thought, she stopped and whirled around, quickly focusing on another, smaller tree. Humming energy skated over her skin as she sent it crashing over the hunters' two SUVs—just for good measure.

Satisfied, she sprinted through the woods, ducking beneath branches until she reached her vehicle, panting with panic. Her heart hammered against her chest so hard she feared it might burst free. The hunters weren't going anywhere anytime soon, but Darius . . .

She'd put nothing past the abilities of a lycan. He was fast. And determined.

If he was free now, he'd be after her soon.

She opened the door and slid behind the wheel. She wasn't about to stick around and give him the chance to catch up with her.

*   *   *

IT WAS LIKE AN earthquake. Everything shook. The house groaned and burst, splitting at the seams, debris flying everywhere. Snow poured inside along with a profusion of branches and tree. The kitchen was gone, flattened.

Screams filled the air. Darius added to them, kicking at the hunter closest to him, cracking his knee with a gratifying crunch. The man dropped with a sharp cry as Darius surged against his chains, ignoring the killing agony of the silver melting skin and sinew. He lunged, jumped, splintering the chair beneath him. Flinging his arms wide, he threw off his chains and slid the restraints down the rest of his body.

Choking down smoke and debris, he covered his mouth. Somewhere a fire crackled and hissed. The air smoldered, making it hard to see his hand in front of him, but he could make out that the roof had caved in on one side of the house. Most of the screams and shouts came from that direction. Among cries of pain and pleas for help from men pinned beneath the rubble, were other urgent cries:

"Where is he?"

"Do you see him?"

"Find him!"

"Look! I think he's over there!"

A hunter charged him and he quickly side-stepped the attack, swiping the man's legs out from under him.

He moved fast, staying low, hugging the floor in case someone sent a silver bullet his way. He moved deeper into the house, into the portion that was still intact. Locating a window, he crashed through it, heedless of the glass.

In a flash, he lost himself in trees. Out of sight, he stopped and watched the chaos left behind. Several of the hunters were outside, exclaiming over their vehicles, flattened beneath another tree. They yelled into cell phones. They had no transportation now, but there'd be more hunters soon, coming to their aid, ready to pick up his trail.

He assessed the damage, eyeing the enormous tree sprawled over half of Tresa's house. The tree looked sturdy, healthy. Perfectly strong enough to support the weight of snow on its branches. No sign of decay. No reason it should have fallen. How had that happened?

Suspicion rooted in his gut. He scanned the tree line, searching for the slightest movement . . . the gleam of midnight hair among the foliage, the flash of whiskey gold eyes. Just the slightest sign that she might still be out there.

Then shouts from the house drew his attention. They were swarming outside now, taking stock of their survivors. A few looked to the trees, weapons at the ready.

He cursed under his breath and drew bitter cold air into his lungs. She wasn't stupid. She wasn't hanging around here. She was gone.

He shook his head. And no way would she have tried to help him. More than likely, she had sent that tree crashing on them in hopes of killing them all.

Even as he told himself this, he knew it wasn't true. She knew no tree could kill him. It would harm the hunters. Not him.

She had helped him.

He didn't want her help. He didn't want to have to reevaluate his opinion of her. He wouldn't.

Grinding his teeth down hard, he took off through the trees.

EIGHT

Tresa's flight to San Vista included a three-hour layover in Seattle, so she had plenty of time to formulate a plan and exorcise thoughts of Darius from her head. It helped knowing he was probably alive and well. Anything else would have left her guilty. She'd created a big enough diversion for him to make his escape. One less thing to weigh down her conscience.

As soon as she left the airport, she checked into a hotel and made use of the phone book in her room. Cranking the air conditioner on high, she changed clothes, donning a tank top. Years in arctic temperatures had apparently left her sensitive to heat.

With pen in hand, she began circling names. She'd decided to start by interviewing the families of the victims. Balthazar's new witch was concentrating her killings in San Vista, so this had to be her home. And if this was her home, then maybe she knew the victims. Maybe she had an ax to grind with them.

Taylor, Hannah and Shannan. Tresa couldn't forget their names. Or their faces. The first one, if not all, had probably been a deeply personal kill for Balthazar's witch.

Just like it had been for Tresa. The first one was very personal—the grudge, the wound so deep that she would bind herself to a demon. She'd hated Etienne Marshan so much at that moment that she'd been blind to everything else.

According to the information she'd found back home, the first victim's name was Shannan Guzak. Seven Guzaks were listed in the phone book. She circled the name of the last one several times. Hopefully one of them was a relation of Shannan's.

Sucking in a deep breath, she dialed the first number. When a voice picked up, she asked for Shannan. *Wrong number.* She dialed the second and third numbers with the same result. At the fourth call, a man answered.

"Hi," she said, her voice cheerful, casual. She swallowed. "Is Shannan there?"

Silence met her. Then the man cleared his throat. His voice came through hoarsely. "Shannan is gone . . . dead . . ."

Bingo. "Oh, I'm so sor—"

The line died in her ear.

Exhaling, she put the phone back on its hook. She may not have gotten the conversation she wanted out of him, but at least she knew where to begin.

She quickly scrawled down the address on a piece of paper and stuffed it into her pocket.

As she moved to leave her hotel room, she spotted her reflection in the mirror. Dark smudges that resembled twin bruises shadowed her eyes. Her whiskey eyes looked enormous in her face. She hadn't slept on the flight down. She grabbed her backpack, slung it over her shoulder and headed to the elevator.

Outside the hotel she paused, adjusting to the sudden warmth. She hadn't been in a warm climate in generations without Balthazar whispering in her ear, controlling her actions, urging her into the dark. She braced herself, instinctively expecting to feel him, hear him.

A breeze lifted the hair off her shoulders, but there was nothing else. No whisper in her ear. No dark, coiling shadow. No Balthazar.

Locating her rental car, she climbed inside and punched the address into the GPS. Pulling out onto the highway, she thought ahead, imagining how she would subtly gather information from the dead girl's family.

She wasn't exactly a people person. She'd been isolated for so long. And she never felt quite right around other people anyway. Not being what she was. It wasn't safe to get close to anyone.

Well, she'd just fake it. Pretend she was someone else. Bottom line, she would do whatever was necessary to get the information she needed to stop Balthazar's witch.

A flash of the last dead girl filled her vision, her eyes glassy with pain and fear.

Tresa blinked and concentrated on the taillights in front of her. To stop *that* from happening again, she had to do whatever it took—even if it meant inviting Balthazar back into her life again. Even if it meant losing herself.

DARIUS STEPPED OUT INTO the warm afternoon. It was pushing eighty degrees in San Vista.

He shrugged out of his jacket and draped it over his shoulder with a frown. It didn't make sense for her to be here, of all places. It wasn't her pattern. And if what she said was true, she was in avoidance of her demon. Considering that this was a prime climate for demons, what was she doing here?

He stuffed his hand in his pocket and brushed paper. On it he'd written down all the information he could remember from browsing the history on her computer. The Rose Petal Killer. San Vista University. It wasn't much to go on, but he was betting this was where she'd gone.

He flagged a cab, stepping back as it nearly rolled up on the curb to reach him. After opening the door, he settled inside and gave instructions for the driver to take him to a hotel.

Leaning back in the seat, he mulled over the witch he'd hunted halfway around the world. She was a mystery. Why she was here, what she was doing, why she had bothered to save him . . . it all bewildered him.

She couldn't be trusted. That much hadn't changed.

Next time when he found her, he wouldn't lose her again.

Tresa fell back on the bed and rubbed her aching eyes, exhausted from her meeting with Shannan's family. It had been hard sitting in that tiny living room with the girl's grandmother, whose too-wise eyes reminded Tresa so much of her own grandmother.

Tresa still remembered Grandmère . . . all these years later. The steel gray of her hair, the palc blue of her eyes that could reach inside you and see everything.

Fortunately, Mary Guzak's eyes hadn't been as discerning as they'd looked to Tresa. They'd hardly stared at her, looking somewhere else, beyond Tresa's shoulder, seeing something else in excruciating detail. Every once in a while that gaze drifted to the photos lining the paneled wall—to a little girl, a bright-eyed Shannan posing with a soccer ball. There were several of these—all the way up until recently, and Tresa guessed that even in college she'd been quite the soccer player.

Tresa rubbed the bridge of her nose. She still didn't have much to go on. She'd pretended to be a college friend of Shannan's. The grandmother had let her in . . . served her iced tea, but Shannan's uncle soon arrived, his gaze suspicious. He'd hovered close to his mother throughout their conversation.

"You went to school with Shannan?" he'd asked.

"Yes. We took an English class together." As Shannan had been a sophomore at San Vista,

Tresa thought it was safe to assume she'd taken an English class sometime during the last few semesters.

Her grandmother hadn't disputed that, merely nodded vacantly.

Tresa wet her lips. "I'm so sorry. Shannan . . ." She shook her head, all words that came to mind so empty, so meaningless. "She didn't deserve this."

Mrs. Guzak nodded, absently running her hands up and down her thighs. Her son, standing several feet away, crossed his arms, watching like a hawk.

Throat dry, Tresa added, "Do the police have any leads?"

Mrs. Guzak shook her head, as if the question confused her. "They don't know . . . they wanted to know if anyone had been bothering Shannan, following her, hanging around her . . . giving her problems . . ."

"Had anyone? Done that?"

"You don't know?" Shannan's uncle replied, his tone seeming to say: *Shouldn't you know? You're her friend.*

"Shannan didn't say. But she's been so busy. Between school, soccer and work, I haven't seen much of her lately. We were supposed to go to dinner—" At this a choked cry burst from Mrs. Guzak's lips. She covered her face with one hand, waving the other apologetically at Tresa.

Her son stepped forward then, placing a hand protectively on her shoulder. "That's enough. This isn't a good time."

"I understand," she mumbled, grabbing her bag. "I'll show myself out."

Her heart twisted as she remembered the conversation. *It was Balthazar's doing.* She knew it. More pain, more heartache and misery. And it wouldn't stop. He wouldn't stop.

She closed her eyes in an anguished blink. He'd never stop as long as he had a new vessel . . . someone willing and malleable. Someone unlike her.

She'd always fought him, resisting his wishes. And she would continue to do that once she made sure this witch was put away where Balthazar couldn't manipulate her anymore.

She swallowed against the sudden bitterness flooding her mouth. The moment he lost his new witch he would be on her like a parasite, sucking her life, her will. Especially if he caught her here, where he flourished.

She forced the prospect from her head. She couldn't think about that. Couldn't let it frighten her. Sighing, she rolled over on the hotel bed, hugging a pillow under her cheek, suddenly tired. The last forty-eight hours were catching up with her.

The fading sunset glowed through the curtains, turning the yellow bedspread to gold. Her eyes drifted shut, her body easing, tension slipping away as she surrendered to sleep.

NINE

He struggles against his binds, his face red with exertion and fury. He's an athlete. His body strong and young, corded with muscles. Muscles you have admired for so long, loving and caressing them with your yearning gaze. Now they're yours. He *is* yours.

You drag the knife against one of his pecs, quivering with tension.

"Stop!" he shouts, jerking against his bindings. "Let me out of here, you crazy bitch."

You smile at him. So strong. So masculine.

With a mind of its own, the knife trails down the flat, shuddering belly. Washboard abs. A powerful body . . . Capable of so much. Defenseless against you.

The knife dips, tracing his manhood as would a lover's mouth. Less impressive than the rest of him, but still nothing to be overlooked. It's so important to him, after all.

"Please." He sobs now, the sounds mingling

with his broken pleas. They always beg so sweetly at the end. A symphony to your ears. The knife kisses his skin, presses deeper, eager for its next meal. Deep moans fill the air.

He's ready.

But not yet. Everything has to be right. A handful of rose petals, soft as satin, trail from your fingers. They fly through the air like a dove's wings and land over the bed, over the beautiful body stretched out for your pleasure.

His head twists and turns, his glassy eyes wide and rolling, scanning the petals that cover and surround him.

"What—"

"Shh." A finger to his lips and he falls silent.

Until the blade plunges deep.

And the true symphony begins again.

TRESA WOKE WITH A scream lodged in her throat. At first she wasn't sure if it was her voice or the vestiges of her nightmare, some echo of that young man's suffering.

She dragged a shaking hand down her face. No nightmare. It was happening now. She knew that. Bile rose in her throat and she lunged for the bathroom. Clutching the seat, she emptied the contents of her stomach, heaving until there was nothing left. Rising, she wiped her face with a hand towel.

Panic hammering in her heart, she staggered into the room and reached for the phone. Without planning what to say, she dialed 911.

At the operator's greeting, she stammered out in a rasping voice, "Hello. Yes. A man is being hurt . . ." She wet her dry lips. "He's being murdered."

"Can you tell me where this is happening, ma'am?"

"I don't—" She pressed a hand to the side of her head.

At her pause, the operator asked, "What's your name, ma'am?"

"I don't know where it's happening exactly," she rushed to say, her mind running back over her dream, seeing the room again, the tiniest details. "I saw a light. Red glowing letters. They blinked. The Hungry Horse. I don't know. Maybe it's a restaurant?" Helpless, she pounded her fist against her thigh and blinked burning eyes.

The sound of keys tapping came through the line, and then the quick, calm voice: "Off Highway 71?"

"Yes, there was a highway." She recalled the roar of trucks in the distance. "Maybe that's it."

"Do you have any more information? Can you describe the victim?"

"He was on a bed. The blinds are to the left of the bed." She sucked in a deep breath and rubbed her forehead, wondering whether she should just go ahead and say it. "It's the Rose Petal Killer. Please help him. He's bleeding—"

"The killer is bleeding, ma'am?"

"No! The victim. The guy on the bed!"

"The man with the knife . . . can you describe him? What's he wearing?"

"Just help him," she cried, desperation thick in her throat, making her voice a hoarse whisper. Her fingers clutched the mouthpiece. "Save him!"

Frustrated and unconvinced that calling 911 had done any good, she hung up the phone and quickly picked it back up, dialing information for the Hungry Horse.

Moments later, directions in hand, she yanked on her shoes and raced out the door. She'd come here to stop Balthazar and his witch. This might be her chance to do that. And maybe she wouldn't be too late.

She was too late.

By the time she found the roadside restaurant that shared a parking lot with a sprawling, run-down motel, police cars and ambulances already swarmed the area. Apparently her call to 911 had been taken seriously. There was even a television van on the scene.

She parked in front of the restaurant and walked to where several other bystanders had gathered, craning their necks, hoping for a view of something to talk about to their friends.

"What's going on?" she asked a guy in a plaid shirt.

He adjusted the John Deere cap on his head. "They're saying some guy's dead in there."

She closed her eyes in a slow, pained blink. "They were too late."

He sent her a curious glance. "What?"

"Police," she amended. "Always too late."

He nodded as though in agreement.

She carefully schooled her expression into mild curiosity. "How'd he die?"

"Heard it was murder." He scratched his bristly jaw and shrugged. "Least I don't think they'd have a dozen cop cars, ambulances and reporters around for some guy who just had a heart attack."

She nodded, and then tensed as she caught sight of one of the news cameras scanning the crowd. For a moment, it seemed like that lens paused on her. All her life, ever since she was cursed, she'd worked hard to stay off the grid.

With a gasp, she spun around. The last thing she needed was her face on the news. Especially after just escaping a lycan and a group of lycan hunters.

Hands shaking, she fumbled with her car keys as she returned to her car. Sliding behind the wheel, she stared bitterly at the flashing lights and mob of people. *Was the killer out there? Balthazar?*

She would have a better chance of catching Balthazar's witch if he didn't know she was here. She felt her lips curl. He must be loving this new one. She was on a roll. Four dead now.

She clenched her hands on the steering wheel. She had to catch the witch before she made it five.

DARIUS WATCHED THE TELEVISION as he waited for the hotel bartender to finish pouring his drink. His fingers drummed an impatient rhythm on the bar, his mind playing over how he might locate Tresa.

He glanced around the dim, mahogany-rich bar as if he might find her here. Across the bar a blonde toyed with her straw and looked at him with coy invitation, hunching her shoulders to maximize the effect of her cleavage. He looked away, back to the television above the bar.

A female like Tresa was hard to forget. It wasn't just her beauty. She possessed a seductive allure . . . Secrets lurked in her eyes. She stood out. He had that going for him, at least.

A reporter was live on the scene, reporting what she called another gruesome murder. He started to look away again from the well-coiffed reporter. He'd had his fill of gruesome murders. He'd had a lifetime of them. He didn't need to hear another one recapped. But then he heard a string of words . . .

The Rose Petal Killer.

His attention snapped back.

. . . *Police won't confirm or deny if this is another death at the hands of the Rose Petal Killer* . . .

He scanned the location printed at the bottom of the screen in block letters and whirled to leave, forgetting all about his drink.

As soon as she returned to her room, Tresa moved fast and changed into more comfortable clothing. As if she could remove the taint of the night's events. Falling into bed, her motivation was simple. She needed to reach Balthazar . . . or his witch. Either one. At the moment, the two seemed interchangeable. As much as she dreaded it, she had to do it.

She breathed slow, deep breaths, relaxing her muscles and easing into sleep.

Unfortunately, no one waited for her in her dreams. Just silent, empty darkness. Peace. Usually the very thing she craved but could never find.

A faint, insistent hammering roused her. Her eyes snapped open to a sharp, persistent knocking.

She blinked and bolted upright, staring uncomprehendingly at her door. Her heart thumped hard against her ribs. Who could it be? She didn't know anyone. And no one knew her here . . .

She rose and peered through the peephole. A man and a woman stood outside her door, both dressed in dark business attire. The man looked left and right, scanning the corridor. The female stared back at the peephole as if she knew Tresa was standing on the other side, watching her. Her nose prickled.

"Yes?" she asked through the door.

"Ms. Morgan?" the female asked, using the

name Tresa had checked into the hotel with. Morgan was the surname she'd used for almost a decade now. It would soon be time to change her last name.

"Yes," she replied.

"I'm Detective Flannery with the San Vista PD." She flashed identification near the peephole. "This is my partner, Detective Simpson. Could we have a few words with you?"

Detectives? A mixture of alarm and excitement rushed through her. They could give her the glimpse into the investigation she needed. But why were they here? How had they found her?

With a deep breath, she unlocked the door. Both detectives looked her up and down, appraising.

"Ms. Morgan?" Detective Flannery was apparently in charge of talking. "May we come inside?"

Tresa waved them in. The door fell shut behind them. She crossed her arms, letting the long sleeves of her sweater drape over her fingers. "What can I do for you?"

The guy, Simpson, finally spoke. "Did you place a phone call from this room at approximately seven forty-five this evening?"

Ice shot through her veins. She knew precisely what phone call they were referring to.

How was she going to explain that? "Maybe. I can't remember."

"You can't remember placing a 911 call?" Flannery asked, her dark eyes cunning and skeptical. She was no one's fool.

Tresa expelled a deep breath, seeing no way out of this. Crossing her arms, she sat on the edge of her bed and looked up at them. There was only one way to play this. "You won't believe me."

"Tell the truth," Flannery commanded.

Tresa's lips quirked and she bit back a snort. "The truth will set you free?" She'd seen plenty of people die miserable deaths over the centuries for telling the truth. She wasn't so naïve.

They stared at her, wearing similar expressions of impatience.

"A man died tonight," Simpson reminded her grimly. As if she needed reminding. She'd been there.

"I'm aware of that."

"Yes," Flannery retorted, her gaze piercing. "And how is it you are aware, Ms. Morgan?"

"I saw it happen." She watched them, certain they would not understand her meaning.

"You were there?" Simpson asked sharply, eagerly, his square jaw hard and unyielding.

She winced. "Not exactly. But I saw it."

The two detectives exchanged looks. "You weren't there but you saw it?" Flannery asked, taking a step closer.

"Look." Tresa waved her hands in the air as if groping for words. "I was just trying to help by placing that call. I don't want to end up in a padded room or anything."

Flannery propped a hand on her hip, exasperated. "We're conducting an investigation into the killing spree of some sicko who doesn't appear to be slowing down. If you're trying to help, then spit it out.

"We can question you here or at the station," Flannery added, her voice hardening. "Your choice."

"I have visions." Not a lie. "I see things, people, events . . . as they're happening."

Simpson muttered beneath his breath, his entire demeanor changing, relaxing. He turned back for the door, but not before she heard his words. "Great. She's a nutcase."

"I know it sounds crazy, but I saw the murder as it happened tonight."

Flannery's gaze remained fastened on Tresa. "You're a psychic."

Not a question. Tresa took that as a good sign. Maybe Flannery had an open mind.

She nodded tightly; it was the easiest explanation. There were plenty of hacks out there who claimed to be clairvoyants. It wasn't a crime. They couldn't prove her wrong and they couldn't arrest her for it.

"And you saw the killer?" Flannery pressed, her dark eyebrows drawing together. "Do you know what he looks like?"

"No. The killer wasn't in my direct view." *Because I was in her mind.* "I watched as—" Tresa caught herself before saying *she*. She didn't want to reveal that much yet. First, she'd see how seriously they took her. "I watched the killer carve him up."

"C'mon, Flan. Let's get back to the station. We're wasting time on this crap." Simpson looked at Tresa scathingly. "She's got nothing."

Flannery sent him a quelling look, clearly unwilling to give up yet. After a moment of silent communication, he sighed and motioned for her to continue the questioning.

The female detective took out a notepad. "How many of these visions have you had?"

"I've had visions of all the other victims, if that's what you're asking. I didn't connect what I was seeing until I saw photos of the victims on the news. That's when I knew these were more than nightmares." Always go with a kernel of truth.

Flannery paused in her writing to stare at her thoughtfully, presumably gauging the truth of this.

Tresa gazed back calmly. This could be her opportunity to prove that she deserved to be included in this investigation. Once that happened, she could ferret out useful information that would help her lead them to the witch to make an arrest. Once the female was behind bars, Balthazar could do little damage through her.

"I haven't seen the killer, but I can describe the scene. And are you sure your killer is a man?" There. She'd said it.

And that got their attention. Simpson looked dubious and Flannery looked expectant. Like she'd better deliver something good or they were out of here.

"Your killer is a woman," she stated.

Flannery looked at her partner sharply.

He looked shocked but tried to hide it, shrugging a shoulder as if she hadn't just said something significant. "How did you know . . ." Simpson's voice faded at Flannery's sharp look.

Tresa cocked her head to the side. "You already knew that?" It hadn't been in the news.

Flannery inclined her head. "We found hairs at the scene. We suspect we're looking for a female. But we haven't released that to the public."

"So you believe me?"

Flannery didn't answer that. "And you know the killer is female . . . because of your visions?"

She knew because witches were female. Instead of saying that, she nodded.

Flannery fished a card out of her pocket. On the back she scrawled a phone number. "You call me day or night with what you see. I don't care how minor the details may be."

Tresa stared steadily into her eyes, trying to see how serious the woman was. Flannery didn't blink. She meant it.

Tresa grasped the cool edge of the card. "I will."

Locking the door behind them, she flipped on the television, glad for the noise in the silence. That was probably what she liked most about TV, why she was grateful for its invention. It filled the awful silences. She could turn it on and not feel quite so alone.

She found a local news station and left it there, hoping for some information about tonight's victim. If her suspicions were correct, the guy had been someone her witch knew. Maybe another student at San Vista University. Watching the screen, she sat on the bed, smoothing her palms over her soft cotton pajama bottoms. This time she didn't jump at the knock at the door, thinking the detectives might have returned with more questions.

A glance through the peephole showed one of the hotel maids. Opening the door, Tresa said, "Yes?"

The woman blinked, as if she didn't know how to respond. Then she looked searchingly to her right. Tresa followed her gaze . . . and gasped at the large shape there.

She tried to slam the door shut, but he was too fast. He grabbed her arm and thrust her inside the room before him, pausing only to lightly pat the maid on the cheek as if they were old friends.

His deep voice rumbled on the air. "Thank you, sweetheart. Forget about me and go back to work now."

She nodded rather dazedly, smiling at Darius with yearning. It was clear she didn't want to go anywhere. She was enamored of the lycan, and not by accident, Tresa was sure. Lycans possessed the ability to enthrall—especially when it came to the opposite sex.

"Go. Now," he commanded.

She moved away.

And then he shut the door. Sealing them in.

She yanked her arm free and stumbled away, rubbing her skin, still feeling the burning imprint of his fingers there.

"You found me," she rasped.

He'd survived. A ripple of relief coursed through her that she quickly squelched. She didn't want him to know she was relieved. The last thing she needed was for him to think she was happy to see him. *She wasn't.*

He crossed his arms and squared off in front of her, blocking the door. "Not too difficult."

"Now what?" she asked, her voice quivering. She lifted her chin. "You cuff me to the bed again? Settle in and wait for a demon?"

He moved from the door, apparently unconcerned that she would bolt for freedom. And why should he worry? She could never outrun him.

Yes, she had powers, abilities. She could bring the ceiling down on him if she wanted to, but did she really want to draw Balthazar to her side with Darius here? No. That was the last thing she wanted to do.

He clasped his hands behind his back and strolled around the room with a calmness that belied the tension swirling in the air. Her gaze swept over him. All lean lines and well-honed muscles, his body was built for conquering.

Or for giving pleasure. She banished the outrageous thought. There was no pleasure to be had at the hands of a lycan.

He stopped beside the window and peered out through the curtains before looking back at her. His silver eyes pinned her. "Did you make that tree fall on the house?"

She snorted and sat on the edge of the bed, suddenly needing to sit—her legs were shaking too badly. "How else did you imagine it happened?"

"Why'd you do it?"

He continued to stare at her, his pewter gaze hot and probing. Her skin tingled where it roamed, and she resisted the urge to fidget.

He moved closer now. One step and he could touch her. A shiver skimmed her spine.

She shrugged one shoulder, uncomfortable beneath that stare, suddenly wishing she was still standing—and farther away from him. "It didn't seem right, leaving you there at their mercy."

"*Right?*" He uttered the word as though he had never heard it before. Clearly he didn't expect her to be concerned with matters of right and wrong. Well, *wrong* maybe.

"As you've pointed out, you are what you are through no choice of your own. It doesn't seem fair that they should kill you for that alone."

"It doesn't?" He gazed at her like she was a curiosity.

"You're not like the other . . ." She couldn't bring herself to say it.

"Lycans," he supplied.

"You're trying to break the curse, however pointless your efforts."

"Such a pessimist." Shaking his head, he moved to the window again and looked down at the parking lot. She took the time to study him unreservedly. The broad expanse of his back; the perfect mold of his jeans over his ass. Heat washed her face.

"What are you doing here?" he asked, still staring out at the night. "These murders interest you. Why?"

She tensed. He knew what had brought her here, and she had to decide how much to tell him since it seemed unlikely that she would shake free of him again. At least not until he realized he was well and truly cursed. Forever. No undoing it.

Because he was as trapped as she was.

TEN

"You want to know why I'm here? Very well. I'll tell you," Tresa said.

At the sound of her silky-smooth voice, he turned and studied her. She held herself tensely, her lithe shape reminding him of a wire stretched taut. Her hair hung sleekly around her face. His palms tingled, itching to touch the strands and feel if they were as silken as they looked. Just the sight of her drove home how dangerous she was.

He knew she was clever. He couldn't trust her—even if she had helped him escape from those hunters.

He lowered himself to the bed beside her, keeping a careful distance. He had no wish to touch her. Well, he did. He had desires, after all, and she was lovely. Alluring. But he wouldn't succumb to the temptation. He couldn't.

She obviously didn't want to be close to him,

either. She scooted inches away, moistening her lips, and his stomach clenched at the sight of that pink tongue tracing her very desirable mouth.

She continued, "I was telling the truth about my demon. He hasn't bothered me in over a year. In the past, even in cold climates, he would make brief appearances and try to regain control over me."

"Go on. What has this got to do with you being here?"

Her lip curled in the semblance of a smile. "I'm here because Balthazar is here."

Everything inside him leapt to life. The very demon who'd granted her wish and started the lycan curse . . . was *here*. He started to push up from the bed, as if he would go find the bastard right then. Her hand on his thigh pulled him back—and that touch drove every thought from his head.

A hissing breath escaped him.

She jerked her hand back, color staining her pale cheeks.

"Don't," he warned.

She nodded quickly, obviously understanding. She'd been around long enough to understand the nature of a lycan—the urges, the lack of impulse control. He'd stopped himself from killing and feeding during the last century, but he didn't live as a monk. Sex was the one vice he allowed himself. Occasionally and with caution.

His thigh burned where her hand had touched him. He looked away, clenching the edge of the bed until he regained his control, wrapping it around him like a shield.

After a moment, he leveled his gaze back on her and got to the matter at hand. "Balthazar. That's his name?"

Her voice floated, whisper soft. "Yes."

"Why did you come looking for him? I thought you wanted to avoid him."

Her throat worked as she swallowed. "I have to stop him. He's found another witch to manipulate. They have to be stopped."

"Ah, such an altruist."

The gold in her eyes flashed like warm candlelight. "Believe me or not. It's the truth."

"Easy," he soothed. "I believe you." And amazingly, he did. She was trying to stop her demon from hurting others. Just like she'd saved him from the hunters. "How do we find him?"

We.

As easily as that, before he'd consciously decided it, he'd already accepted that they were in this together. They were going to have to team up to hunt down this demon.

She stared at him with wide eyes. Apparently she hadn't missed the *we,* either.

"Like I said, he's found another witch. Someone willing to commit depravities. So he's not eager to reconnect with me now."

He stared at her, the puzzle pieces fitting together. "She's the Rose Petal Killer."

Tresa nodded. "I've been in her head when she does these horrible things. My bond to Balthazar puts me there. I'm there, but I can't see her. I don't know who she is."

"But you're a witness to the killings." He absorbed that. "We can figure this out. We can find her." And when they found her, they'd find the demon.

She nodded, sliding her hands nervously along her thighs.

The motion seemed so . . . human. Something a normal woman would do when she was nervous. Those slim fingers held his attention too long. He remembered the pressure of her hand on his thigh and his gut tightened.

He blinked and looked away, struggling to reconcile what was before him with what he had created in his head.

Standing, he moved to the phone and dialed

the front desk. "Yes. We're going to need to move into a larger room. Two beds. Tonight if possible."

After listening to the clerk, he hung up the phone and faced her. "Gather your things."

She hesitated only a moment and he knew the wheels were spinning in her head. She was trying to decide whether to fight him on this.

At last she reached a decision. The right one, apparently, because she nodded jerkily and gathered a few things. Moving into the bathroom, she returned with a small striped cosmetic bag that she stuffed into her luggage. A quick look around confirmed that she'd left nothing else. "I'm ready."

Was her seeming malleability another ploy? Would she try to escape the first chance that came along?

She sighed beneath his scrutiny. "I'm not going to run." Evidently her powers extended to mind reading. "All I want to do is find Balthazar's witch and stop her. As long as you don't get in my way, then we won't have any problems."

"Then we won't have any problems," he agreed, lifting her luggage. "We're both after the same thing."

For now, they were in this together.

Her mouth curled humorlessly. "Who would ever have thought that possible?"

She glided past him and out the door. Shaking his head, he followed her into the hall, marveling that he should feel anything less than hatred for her.

But it was there. A decided lack of animosity for this witch who would delay her own escape to save him. Who wanted to stop another witch from taking innocent lives.

He stared at her slim back, ramrod straight. She strode ahead of him with effortless grace. Her hips swayed in a way that beckoned him, called to the animal inside him that craved a mate—the carnal, savage part that wanted to seize her hips, pull her beneath him and drive his cock deep into her heat. And maybe most alarming, it wasn't just about claiming her, fucking her until the urge was gone.

She was a mystery, and he felt compelled to solve her. He shouldn't feel that way, but the urge was there—to peel back all her layers, to see to the true core of her. And he couldn't even tell himself not to care. Not as long as solving the riddle of who she was—*what* she was—helped him reclaim his soul.

* * *

DARIUS TURNED ON THE television as soon as they entered the room, flipping channels until he found the local news.

She dropped her bag beside one bed, staring at the short distance to the other one and wondering how she was supposed to sleep at night with him so close, her senses full of him. *Feeling him. Smelling him.* She shook her head. A lycan, a predator, a creature known for low impulse control. She was a fool to let him affect her.

To occupy her hands, she started unpacking. The murder was all over the news. They were reporting on the few details released and interviewing people who knew the victim, most of them students at San Vista College. Just like the last four victims had been. Fear was clear in their faces. They were worried. The reporter featured a few university parents who talked about withdrawing their children.

She paused, watching, sick at heart by the evidence of so much pain, so much damage left by Balthazar. "All the victims have been students at San Vista College."

He glanced back at her from where he sat on a small couch before the television. "Then we know where to start."

Tresa nodded. "She knows all the victims.

Personally." She thought back to her dreams, tapping into the thoughts and emotions of the witch in those moments when she killed. "She's connected to them. I wouldn't be surprised if they're in her circle of friends."

On the television, the dean of students was making a speech on the steps of a campus building. He expressed his grief and invited students to a memorial service tomorrow.

"She'll be there," Tresa announced, certain. "She won't be able to stay away."

"Then we'll be there, too." He rose in one fluid motion, stripping his shirt over his head smoothly.

Her breath seized inside her lungs. How long had it been since she'd been alone with a man? In such close quarters? His skin was swarthy, olive hued. His body sculpted perfectly.

Her belly fluttered treacherously. Her gaze devoured him, her chest aching, tight, as he moved into the bathroom and started the shower.

She swallowed past the sudden dryness in her mouth.

He emerged again, every masculine inch of him exuding power and virility. Her palms grew damp and she sank down on the edge of the bed, sliding her hands under her thighs, trapping them as if she didn't trust them not to reach for him.

He rummaged in his bag and reemerged with a pair of handcuffs.

She gasped and recoiled, springing up and fleeing to the far corner of the room.

He angled his head, his eyes hard and intent. Merciless still, even now that they'd teamed up. It was an unpleasant reminder that nothing had really changed. Not him. Not what he thought of her.

He clenched his jaw. "You want to do this on the bed or the chair?"

She shook her head. "Not again." She held up a hand to ward him off. "You said we're in this together—"

"That doesn't mean I can trust you."

"What am I going to do? Run away? Where am I going to go? You know why I came here. I can't hide from you anymore."

He approached. She backed into the wall until she could go no farther.

He grasped her wrist, positioning the steel cuff over it. She cringed and tried to pull free, but the hot press of his fingers was inescapable.

He studied her. His face was so close. *He* was so close. The manly scent of him filled her nostrils.

"I can't afford to take the chance." He actually sounded apologetic.

"Please." Her voice cracked, her gaze dropping to the cuffs. Memories flooded her, as fresh as though they'd happened yesterday. They flashed through her mind like bursts of lightning in the dark. The weight of a chain squeezing around her. The burn of water in her nose, in her lungs. "I can't be bound. Not again."

He cocked his head as though he understood she wasn't simply referring to when he had handcuffed her. But something else. Something worse. His gaze pierced her, penetrating, demanding elaboration . . . the truth, *everything*.

She swallowed, words choking her. Shaking her head, she looked away, blinking suddenly stinging eyes, unwilling to bare herself to him.

The past was her burden. She'd never spoken of it . . . never shared it with anyone. Not in all this time. But then, who would she share such a horrible memory with? Who cared enough to want to know? There was no one. There had never been anyone in all these years.

"It was Etienne Marshan," she heard herself begin, her voice a whisper.

Impossible as it seemed, his silver eyes brightened. Of course he recognized the name. "The first lycan . . . the one you cursed?"

"Yes." She nodded. "He was my liege lord. He bound me, weighed me down with chains and stones." She drew a deep breath. "And then he drowned me." She could almost taste the dark river water again, feel it gagging her, blacking out her world.

Darius gazed at her, unblinking. "He tried to kill you?"

"He did kill me," she retorted. "I died that day. My heart. My body." She thrummed her fingertips against her mouth, nervous energy zipping through her as she recalled that day . . . that nightmare she relived whenever she allowed herself to remember. Which wasn't often.

But she relived it again right now, sharing it with Darius. She didn't understand why she was telling him this, only that it felt right. She needed him to understand. Needed him to know why she couldn't be restrained again. Also . . . she needed him to understand that she wasn't what he thought. She was more.

He watched her with his piercing gaze, waiting for her to continue. She moistened her lips. His gaze lowered, fixing on her mouth with an intensity that made her skin tighten.

"He murdered me alongside my family that day. When Balthazar promised me vengeance, I took it. With my last dying breath, I took it. I didn't realize what it would mean . . . what he would do." She laughed brokenly, bitterness welling up inside her. "Demons are tricky that way. He caught me at my weakest moment. I wasn't in a position to read the fine print. I just wanted to make Marshan pay."

She released her breath and dropped her gaze to the cuffs he held in his hand. He didn't move toward her. His legs stayed braced squarely in front of her. She held herself tightly, waiting for the cold steel to circle her wrists.

It never happened.

He touched her chin with his fingers, lifting her face with that gentle contact. His expression was inscrutable, the sharp angles and carved lines revealing nothing.

Everything, her entire world in that moment, centered on his hand on her face. The brush of his fingers against her skin. How long since she had felt the touch of another? Tenderness?

She blinked as he slid his hand away, telling herself it couldn't have been gentleness. He hated her. He wanted her dead. Wanted her to pay, to suffer. She was *his* Etienne Marshan.

And she could not fault him for that.

After a long moment, he tossed the cuffs on the bed and moved into the bathroom without a word, shutting the door.

Alone, she stared at the handcuffs and then the closed bathroom door, marveling that he'd decided to trust her.

She pushed from the wall and turned off the suite's overhead light. Next, she flipped on the small desk lamp. A dull circle of light glowed from beneath the shade.

Tugging back the covers, she slid into the bed nearest the window, positioning her back to the bathroom so she didn't have to see him when he emerged. For some reason, she couldn't stop shivering.

Several minutes passed and she heard the water shut off. Closing her eyes, she feigned sleep. A few moments later, the door opened. That fresh, warm-water smell swept inside the room. She inhaled, catching his clean, soapy scent. Beneath that was the inherent, intoxicating male musk of him. Her chest swelled with a deep breath.

His movements were silent and her back itched, tingled, imagining his gaze there. She longed to turn and take a peek. Instead, she curled more tightly into herself, tried to make herself as small as possible, and resisted the urge.

The desk lamp snapped off, plunging the room into darkness, and all of her senses jumped into hyper-alertness.

A faint spring creaked, the only indication that he'd gotten into his bed. She envisioned that bare chest exposed above the sheet. Was he wearing shorts? Boxers? *Anything?*

This was just because she'd isolated herself too much. The unremitting loneliness . . . going without a man's touch . . . without *sex*. That explained why she would yearn for a lycan who justifiably hated her.

"Good night." His voice rumbled across the dark, stroking her flesh as softly as a feather.

She jammed her eyes tightly shut, even though he couldn't know she was only pretending to be asleep.

He couldn't know that it took hours for exhaustion to claim her, with thoughts of him flooding her, consuming her, drowning her just as that river had.

Only instead of the black river water, it was his brilliant silver eyes that she saw.

Eleven

The elevator dings and you step off. An empty corridor looms left and right, cast in yellowy light from the wall sconces. The elevator doors whoosh softly shut at your back. You step right, the plush carpet deadening your steps as you advance. Doors drift past until you reach the one you seek. The door's gold-scripted numbers confirm you're in front of the correct room. You flatten your palm against the wood, imagine you can feel a pulse in the dead particles.

A sigh trembles from your lips as you imagine her on the other side. The one like you. Even now, asleep, she's with you, sharing in everything. You know this. Your hand slides away.

A quick glance left and right reveals you're still alone in the corridor. The faint sound of a television plays from behind the door of a nearby room.

You squat in front of the door and deposit the bunch of rose stems. Stems minus their blooms. A slow smile curves your lips as you recall how you used those petals. Even now Jason flashes before your eyes, the pink petals arranged so gloriously around his body. He was more beautiful in that moment than ever in life, and you're sad . . . because it's over. And you can't do it again. At least to him.

With one last glance at the butchered roses, you step back, satisfied that your token will be waiting there for her when she wakes up.

TRESA'S EYES FLEW WIDE. Darkness swirled around her, thick as tar. Her face turned instinctively toward the door. A small thread of light glowed from underneath.

"She's here." She barely breathed the words but she felt Darius instantly alert, fully understanding and springing from the bed.

Light flooded the room as he yanked the door open. Beyond his naked torso, Tresa could detect nothing. No one. But she knew the other witch had just been there. Standing there, staring at their door. A shiver scraped down her spine to know that she had been so close. That she still was. She couldn't have gotten far. She pushed back her shoulders and forced herself not to tremble like a scared child.

"Hey! You there!" A curse exploded from Darius and he suddenly flew from the room. Tresa dove from the bed and caught the door, stepping into the corridor to see where he was going.

Pain stabbed the bottom of her foot, and she hopped back just as she glimpsed Darius slamming through the stairwell door. A glance down revealed a pile of thorny rose stems.

She examined the bottom of her foot where several of the thorns had pricked her flesh. Blood welled from the puncture wounds. With a muttered epithet, she looked back up. The witch had just stood here. Had left the destroyed flowers while she and Darius slept. This time there was no stopping the shiver from coursing through her.

She tentatively rested her foot on the floor, stepping over the flower stems to peer down in the direction Darius had fled.

As the seconds ticked by, her heart hammered faster. When a hand closed over her shoulder, she jumped back and screamed.

Darius held both hands in the air as though proclaiming himself safe. Innocent.

"Where'd you come from?" she panted.

He motioned behind him. "There's a second stairwell around the corner."

Her heart rate gradually dropped into the normal realm as disappointment filled her. "You didn't catch her."

"I thought I heard someone in the stairwell . . . running feet." He shook his head. "I went down and back up, but didn't see anyone. It's possible she went into a room."

That seemed likely. The witch couldn't have outrun him—not a lycan.

He bent and gathered the rose stems. "Guess she left these for you."

"She knows I'm here," she said hollowly. The stems had been a message. A warning or a taunt. Maybe both.

He nodded, his gaze locking with hers. "Then so does he."

Tresa swallowed past the unbearably thick lump in her throat. Balthazar could take her, claim her at any moment. Whenever the mood struck him.

Darius looked satisfied. Of course. He was only here to hunt her demon. He didn't care what happened to her.

Deflated, she turned back for the room, wincing when she stepped down.

"What's wrong?" His hand grasped her arm.

"Nothing. Just stepped on those." She waved a disgusted hand at the butchered roses.

"Let me see."

She tried to object, but his warm hand slid around her calf. She grabbed hold of his shoulder with both hands for balance. Immediately her hands were full of warm male skin, silk over steel. His muscles bunched and rippled beneath her palms. Her breath seized inside.

She didn't even feel him prodding at the sole of her bare foot. She only felt the powerful body in her hands. The heady aroma of him as soap and man wafted to her nose. Her feminine parts tightened and clenched, reminding her that it had been a long, long time since a man had touched her. Longer since one had been inside her, filling her, moving hard and fast to satisfy her body's deepest aches.

"You're bleeding."

Suddenly she was off her feet. He swung her into his arms as if she were nothing more than a feather. He lowered her onto his bed, which only made her more uncomfortable. She was drowned in the scent of him, awash in a sea of sheets still warm from his body. His gaze skimmed over him. *His amazing body.*

Her mouth watered and she forced her gaze away from the ridged muscles of his belly.

"I'll clean it." He moved toward the bathroom. She heard running water.

"It's hardly going to kill me," she muttered when he returned with a wet washcloth.

His lips twisted into the semblance of a grin. He propped her legs across his lap, her foot on his thigh. His fingers on her ankle sent shock waves up her leg and she squirmed. As the seconds passed, she grew more and more tense beneath his careful attention.

The washcloth stilled against the soles of her feet. His silver eyes fastened on her face, peering at her in that intent way of his, impossible to read.

And yet there was something different in those eyes. His eyes glowed brightly . . . more potent than usual.

"Sorry," he murmured, his voice velvet deep.

He thought he'd hurt her? She wasn't even aware of her injuries anymore. There could be thorns embedded in her flesh and she wouldn't feel it. She only felt his hand on her ankle, heard the steadiness of his breath, smelled the scent of him.

"Does that hurt?" He probed a particularly tender area of her foot.

"No."

His fingers skimmed the bottom of her foot, rounding over the top. "What about here?"

"No." Her breath caught, her chest lifting sharply.

His hand roamed on, fingertips dancing up her calf, gliding over her knee. His touch stopped, brushing the sensitive inside of her knee. "Here?"

She shook her head, beyond words, afraid that if she made the slightest sound he would hear his effect on her. That she wanted him. Desire pumped hot and heavy through her, making her limbs feel heavy as lead.

He inched closer, his gaze hot on her. His warm breath fanned the side of her face. Helpless, she lifted her face to his, seeking, yearning. His nose brushed her cheek. She knew his lips were there, close, but she couldn't feel them.

His fingers stroked the sensitive skin beneath her knee. "So nothing hurts?" His voice teased the tiny hairs near her ear. "But you're shaking."

Everything inside her trembled. She wanted to turn into his arms, to curl up against him. She wanted to wrap her arms around his neck and feel all that warm male skin against her, and remember what it was to be a desirable woman.

He brushed the hair off her neck.

"I'm not shaking." She leaned forward to get up, desperate to put some space between them.

His fingers closed around her arm and

pulled her back down on the bed, then he leaned over her.

Everything inside her seized, tightened with expectation, with dread, hope. *Want.*

But his lips didn't so much as graze hers. His face hovered directly over hers. Their eyes locked and she could practically count each one of his dark eyelashes fanning out from the brilliant silver.

"Liar," he finally announced. "You're trembling."

A breath shuddered past her mouth, and he swallowed it, finally claiming her lips, diving into the kiss.

They savored it, sampling each other's lips with a thoroughness, a leisure that made her chest ache from the unexpected tenderness, the seductive slide of his tongue against her own.

He drank in her moan, his hand on her thigh now, the callused pads of his fingers an exciting rasp on her skin. He could have her now. She knew it. The way she fell into the kiss, the way her thighs parted for his drifting hand . . .

He knew it, too. Which was why she gasped, reaching for him with groping hands when he pulled away. She choked out his name, quickly sitting up.

He wiped a hand over the back of his mouth

as though he needed to wipe the taste of her from him. The gesture stung.

Everything inside her wanted to call him back, wanted to pull him to her so that she could feel warm again—*alive*. She'd forgotten the wonder of it all. The closeness of another, a kiss so obliterating, so consuming that it washed away all numbness.

He glanced at her and then looked away. Grabbing his shirt, he hurriedly pulled it over his head. She watched, her throat tightening.

"I'll be back in a while," he muttered and fled the room.

Alone, in the center of the bed, she wondered what had just happened. How had she allowed a lycan bent on destroying her to kiss her? How had she liked it? Wanted it?

How could she want him still?

Darius walked without direction, but with purpose. If he moved fast enough, maybe he could outrun his feelings, his desires. The sight of Tresa as he'd left her, warm and welcoming on that bed, her eyes clouded with desire, filled his head. He walked faster.

He left the hotel behind, losing himself in the night's darkness, moving too quickly for anyone to process, becoming nothing more than wind. Briefly, his mind touched on Balthazar, another shadow winding through the night.

No. He wasn't like that. Nothing like that.

He slowed to a stop and looked around. He was in a high-end shopping center, the stores all closed for the night. The lights of a wine bar spilled out on the sidewalk. Two laughing women tripped out the doors as he strode past, one almost bumping into him.

He steadied the blonde, stopping her from colliding into him. Her perfume surrounded him.

"Oh, hello there." She blinked large blue eyes up at him. A slow smile curved her wine-stained lips. She moved lightly on her feet, brushing against him. "Aren't you the gallant gentleman?" Her eyes gleamed at him in invitation, looking him up and down appreciatively. Her friend giggled.

For a moment, his hand lingered on her arm as he toyed with the idea of finishing with this female what he'd started with Tresa.

As soon as the thought entered his mind, he dismissed it. It wouldn't be right.

She wouldn't be Tresa.

Disgusted with himself, he stepped around the woman and continued on, wondering when she had come to consume his thoughts . . . when she had come to mean so much?

Twelve

The Salty Bean was a coffee shop a few miles from the college. Following the memorial service, they decided to check it out, since Shannan had worked there. It was a popular campus hangout, so in Tresa's mind it was a wise use of their time.

If her hunch was right about Balthazar's witch being a student, maybe she frequented the place, too. Tresa winced. Or maybe it was safe to assume she would be there because *she* was. The witch had now proved herself to be aware of Tresa's movements.

A vase full of white lilies sat on a back counter, surrounded with snapshots of all the victims. Jason was wearing a rugby uniform, a ball tucked under his arm. Even from where she sat, his smile was blinding, infectious. Hard to equate him with the young man from her nightmare.

She brought her latte to her lips and sipped

the hot brew. "I'm thinking it's not much of an assumption to say she's a college student, too." Tresa nodded to the shrine. For some reason, it was easier to look at that than at Darius. After he had run out following their kiss last night, she hadn't wanted to meet his gaze. "Just like the other victims."

From the corner of her eye, she observed him lift one shoulder in a shrug. "Yes, I'd say she's affiliated with the school. She could be a professor, though, or someone on staff. Administration."

"Possibly," she agreed before falling silent to absorb everything inside the cozy coffee shop, eavesdropping on the conversations around her. Several times, the topic turned to the murders.

She scanned faces. They were afraid, but titillated, too. They either knew one of the victims, or someone they knew knew a victim. It was gossip—plain and simple.

"She's the one who worked here." Tresa nodded to Shannan's photo.

Darius followed her gaze to the photo before looking back at her. "So. When she died, what did—"

"I don't want to talk about it." Her gaze skittered off him again.

He set his coffee cup down with a clink. "I'm only asking because it might shed some light on who it is we're looking for. I wouldn't have thought you so squeamish. Not after all you've done . . . all you've seen."

He would always throw that in her face. He would never see anything else when he looked at her.

She angled her head sharply and forced her attention back on him. "I guess you don't know me as well as you think you do."

He cupped his coffee with both hands and leaned forward, closer, across the small black-topped table. "I guess not."

His ready admission startled her. Maybe it startled him, too. Or at least left him uncomfortable. He leaned back in his chair for a moment, his cheeks flushed a bit, and then abruptly rose, moving to the back counter, scanning the memorial shrine and the bulletin board on the wall behind it.

She couldn't help noticing the college girls checking him out, their gazes sliding over the long length of him in admiration. He was either oblivious to their glances or indifferent. It would be hard not to notice the way they gawked.

"Hey." A girl stretched over from her chair

to tug on the hem of Tresa's shirt. "Is that your boyfriend?" She nodded to Darius.

Appallingly, she felt tempted to say he was. To claim him, to pretend last night had been real and had meant something.

"No," she said.

"Excellent." The girl gave a catlike smile and rose from her chair. Smoothing her snug tunic top down her hips, she sauntered over to where Darius stood.

Tresa watched the roll of her hips, an uncomfortable knot forming in the pit of her stomach.

"Not very subtle, is she?" a voice asked, drawing Tresa's attention to the guy sharing the table with the girl who was stalking Darius like a jungle cat.

She shrugged as if it didn't matter, plucking at the cardboard sleeve around her cup.

The guy continued, "She's shameless that way. And he's a good-looking guy." He shrugged again, implying that the girl couldn't be held accountable.

"Yeah." Tresa didn't know what else to say. "He is."

"Yeah," he echoed. "And she's the sluttiest girl I know."

Tresa blinked. "Excuse me?"

He grinned and shoved his dark-rimmed glasses up his nose. He managed to look stylish and cute in them. They complemented the handsome roundedness of his features. "She's my cousin, so I can say it. It's nothing I wouldn't say to her face." He extended a hand for Tresa to shake as he picked up his cup and dropped down into the chair across from her. "Name's Carson."

She shook his hand. "Tresa."

"Ooh, exotic. Where are you from? I hear an accent."

She blinked again, taken aback by his openness. She stared at him, wondering how he had come to sit at her table with her saying so few words, and why she felt so comfortable with him. "Luxembourg." That was the relative area where she had been born.

"Cool." He nodded slowly, his bottle-bleached hair so stiff it didn't move in the slightest. "So what brings you here? You a student?"

"Just visiting."

"San Vista? Really? Why would you want to visit here? There are so many cooler places to be."

A shadow fell over them. "Tre."

She looked up to find Darius staring down

at Carson, his glittering eyes intense and disapproving. She scowled back at him. Wasn't she doing what they'd set out to do? Talking to people and gathering information.

"This is Carson." Tresa's gaze skimmed the brunette who stood close to Darius. She motioned at her. "And you've met his cousin already . . ."

"Erin," the girl quickly supplied, looking pleased that Carson had infiltrated their table. She grabbed her half-eaten chocolate muffin and cold drink—some coffee-colored concoction piled high with whipped cream and chocolate drizzle—and dropped down into one of the remaining chairs.

She took a bite of her muffin and smiled up at Darius. Tresa snorted, positive he had that effect on the female population in general. And only partly because he was a lycan and had that whole ability-to-mesmerize thing going for him. He was gorgeous. Plain and simple. Plus, he had that that mysterious edge that drew females like bees to the honeypot. The wounded-warrior type, seeking something, someone, to save him. Somehow she thought that was *him* and had nothing to do with his lycan nature.

In truth, she supposed he *was* all of that.

A man seeking his soul, his redemption. She started with a sudden realization: not that different from her.

Darius looked at Tresa questioningly.

She shrugged, too rattled in her thoughts to consider these two students taking over their table. But she should pay attention. They seemed like regulars here, the very place Shannan had worked. Maybe they'd even known her . . . or the other victims.

Darius lowered his large frame into a wooden chair. He lifted his coffee and took a cautious sip, observing the two cousins who had barged into their midst.

"So I'm guessing you're not a student, either?" Carson asked him, crossing his legs.

Darius glanced at Tresa, clearly wondering what she had shared.

Deciding they weren't going to get anywhere without more directness, Tresa plunged ahead. "We're looking into the murders."

Carson leaned forward, his eyes alight with intrigue. "Are you cops?"

"No."

Erin looked her over, her gaze more skeptical. "Then what are you?"

Tresa hesitated only a moment, considering her next words. "I'm a psychic." Why not?

It was how she'd represented herself to the police, after all.

Erin's and Carson's eyes widened and they exchanged looks. "Cool," Carson breathed.

Erin tossed a lock of brown hair over her shoulder. "So, what . . . you talk to the dead or something? Like in that TV show?"

"No." Tresa took a slow sip, not about to elaborate. Let the little twit wonder.

Erin rolled her eyes. "Sure you do." She swung her gaze to Darius. Her eyes softened. "What about you? You a freak-show, too?"

"No," he answered, his lip faintly curling, and Tresa knew he didn't like the freak-show jab. If the girl knew he was a lycan, she would run screaming from the room.

"Good," she purred. "I didn't think so."

"I'm her—" His eyes captured Tresa's and clung for a long moment.

She held her breath, wondering what he was going to say.

"Partner," he finished.

Well, that was . . . clinical. Professional. For the best.

Erin smiled brightly. Apparently Darius had passed some kind of test. She scooted her chair a little closer, cozying up to him. "What does that mean? You her boss or something?"

"Or something." His gaze slid from Tresa to Erin, leveling her with his hypnotic silver eyes. "Maybe you can help us."

She propped her chin on her fist, her expression a bit dazed. "I'd love to help you."

Tresa shook her head, disgusted at how easily he'd caused the girl to be enamored of him. *Damn lycan*. And it *was* disgust. Not jealousy.

She glanced at Erin's cousin, who also watched with a rapt expression. Lycan magnetism. It wasn't magic exactly. Just some serious charm.

Why hadn't Darius used his magnetism on her? Or maybe he had. She blinked at the sudden thought. Maybe that's why she couldn't stop thinking about him last night, shirtless, his hands on her legs, his mouth on hers, his tongue . . .

Her breath caught and her stomach dipped at the memory. Maybe that's why she'd broken down and acted on her impulses, surrendered to her desires with him.

And yet somehow she knew he hadn't manipulated her—if he even could. That would be too easy an excuse for her wanton behavior last night. If he controlled her actions, she wouldn't feel so guilty, wouldn't be beating herself up for wholeheartedly falling into that kiss with him. He had been the one to stop them from going any further, after all. That didn't seem like the behavior of someone putting her in his thrall.

Darius touched the back of Erin's hand with one finger as he talked. Something tightened in Tresa's chest and she fidgeted uncomfortably on her chair as she observed the flirtation. Part of her wanted to get up and walk away, escape whatever it was she felt. The other part of her wanted to snatch his hand off the girl.

She told herself it was because she wanted to protect the unsuspecting female. Not because she felt possessive. He was flirting with the girl to establish a connection and ferret out information. That was all.

The college girl looked down at Darius's finger on the back of her hand. The tip of her tongue slowly traced her lip and Tresa knew she was imagining more than his finger on her.

He talked to her, his voice low, seductive. "All the victims were college students. Did you know any of them?"

"Sure. I knew Jason. His frat house has all the best parties. Everyone knew him. And Shannan worked here." She gestured to the room. "She played soccer. Every guy on campus wanted to get with her."

Tresa absorbed this information. It seemed as if all the victims were well-known to others. So it seemed doubtful that Balthazar's witch was killing randomly.

These were people who had pissed her off somehow. Legitimately or not, she felt they had wronged her. And someone out there probably knew that about her.

"Jason's frat is having a party tonight in Jason's honor. Like a memorial for him. You should come." The girl flicked her glance to Tresa. "You can bring her, too. Maybe she'll sniff out the killer." Her mouth twisted as if this was almost funny.

"Yeah," Carson seconded. He leaned forward, looking directly at Tresa, his expression urging. "Big white house at the end of Academy Drive. You can't miss it."

Tresa nodded, looking at Darius, seeing in his face that he, like her, thought it was a good idea to attend. "Yeah. We'll go."

Leaning back in her chair, a sharp sense of relief rolled through her. The witch would undoubtedly be there tonight; she wouldn't be able to stay away. Tresa would know her when she saw her, and soon this would be over.

She ignored that other feeling lurking beneath the relief. *Fear.*

Because facing this witch meant facing Balthazar again. And that could mean losing herself all over again.

Thirteen

The detectives were waiting in the lobby when Tresa and Darius returned to the hotel. Darius tensed beside her as Simpson and Flannery stepped in their path.

"Detectives," she greeted them, so he immediately knew who they were and didn't unleash himself on them.

"Ms. Morgan." Flannery looked Darius over carefully, sizing him up.

"You're back." Tresa crossed her arms. "Changed your mind about me? Decided I'm not a fraud, after all?"

"Maybe." Simpson's expression didn't give a hint of his thoughts. "We'd like you to come with us to look at some photos."

"You have a suspect, then?" Darius asked.

"Who are you?" Simpson took a step forward, lifting his chest in that way men did when they were trying to look intimidating.

Darius jerked his head toward her. "A friend."

"We'll drive," Flannery interjected, as if it was decided.

Darius looked down at Tresa. She shrugged and fell in step behind the detectives. They led the way, not speaking until all four of them were in the car and heading across town.

"Where you two from?" Simpson broke the silence to ask.

Tresa slid Darius a look and answered for herself. "Alaska."

"Long way from home," Simpson murmured, tapping the steering wheel.

Tresa stared at Flannery's profile. Even without an ounce of makeup, she was attractive. The soft angles of her face made her age hard to determine. Tresa placed her somewhere in her late twenties.

"Why do you want to talk to me?"

After a shared look with her partner, Flannery answered, "We found DNA on the victim. And a hair."

"Confirming your killer is female."

"C'mon. Tell us how you really knew we were looking for a woman," Simpson demanded, looking back at her in the rearview mirror. He still thought she was full of shit.

She snorted and looked out the window. "I told you how. You just don't want to accept that."

She didn't need them to believe her. They were taking her to the police station, where she could learn more, maybe see some of the evidence they had. Maybe she would even see a photo of the witch responsible for so much pain. Tresa hoped that would be enough to recognize her.

The station was crowded when they arrived, and she wondered if it had anything to do with the murders or if this was just business as usual. Phones rang and bodies rushed around.

"Busy," Darius murmured, apparently thinking the same thing.

"We've got everyone working overtime. We set up a tip line. San Vista isn't the type of place to get a lot of serial killers." Simpson looked at Tresa as he said this. Strangely, she felt that there was accusation in his gaze.

Flannery led them to her desk and motioned to the chair beside it. "You can wait here, sir."

Darius looked from the chair to the detective. "Where are you taking her?"

Unease trickled down Tresa's spine.

"Just that room over there." Flannery motioned to a door.

"Any reason I can't accompany her?"

The two detectives exchanged looks.

"Is that an interrogation room?" Tresa demanded, suddenly knowing that she wasn't here simply to look at photographs. "You want me to go in there? With you?"

At their silence, she pressed. "Are you planning to interrogate me or show me some pictures? Which is it?"

They stared at her blankly.

"I'm such an idiot." She snorted in disgust, crossing her arms over her chest. "Why did you really bring me here? Are you arresting me?"

"No. They're not." Darius took her hand and started to pull her back toward the door. "Let's go."

Simpson slapped a hand on his arm. "Hold on a minute."

Darius stilled and looked at that hand on his arm. "Take your hand off me," he threatened in a low voice, so deep and menacing, unlike the way he'd even spoken to Tresa the day they'd first met. And he'd terrified her then.

Slowly, his stare lifted and the two of them looked at each other intently. Darius's eyes glittered brightly, like stars in a dark night.

"Darius," she murmured, worried that he might actually start growling like a beast there in the police station.

Simpson let go of his arm, and Tresa released the breath she hadn't even realized she was holding.

She turned her glare on Flannery. She was the more reasonable of the two detectives, and Tresa felt the most betrayed by her. "You didn't have to trick me," she snapped. "I'm trying to help you and this investigation, and now you're treating me like I'm a suspect."

"Nothing *like* about it," Simpson drawled, leaning a hip against the desk and crossing his arms over his chest.

Her temper rose, getting the better of her. For some reason she saw all those faces again, so many years ago . . . friends, neighbors, looking at her with condemnation, smirks on their faces, ready to loop the noose around her neck. They reminded her of these detectives.

Flannery copied her partner's pose, crossing her arms. "You were right. Our suspect *is* a woman. A witness saw Jason Morris enter the hotel with a woman." She looked her up and down assessingly. "A woman about your build. Brown hair."

Tresa stared at her, unable to speak as the implication sank in.

They thought she was the killer.

Simpson picked up where Flannery had left off. "A simple lineup with our witness can clear up this whole matter . . ."

"She's not doing it," Darius stated, his voice flat.

"Why? She got something to hide?"

Darius tugged her closer to his side. "Under what circumstances did this witness view this female with Jason Morris? At night? From the back? Across a parking lot? Was she drinking? Had a beer or wine with dinner maybe?"

At the questions, Flannery looked uncomfortable, Simpson just annoyed.

"That's what I thought." Darius took her hand. His broad hand swallowed hers, warm and solid, the sensation comforting.

"Am I under arrest?" Tresa asked.

Finally, grudgingly, Flannnery replied, "No."

"Come on." With a pull of his hand, Darius led her toward the doors.

She dug in her heels and turned, staring directly at Detective Flannery. "Check the airlines. I've only been in town two days. If I killed Jason Morris, then who killed the other victims? Every minute you waste looking at me, you lose hunting the killer who's out there getting ready to strike again."

Because Balthazar wasn't satisfied. He couldn't ever be satisfied. His hunger for the misery of others was voracious.

Darius tugged on her hand and she followed him out of the police station.

*   *   *

TRESA STARED OUT THE backseat window of the cab, hands tucked between her knees. The seat creaked beneath Darius as he leaned forward to glimpse her face. Her eyes, wide and unblinking, scanned the streets they flew past.

He leaned back, uncomfortable with the notion that she might be sad or upset. That she could even feel such normal human emotions was still something he struggled to accept. Even after last night and having lost his head over her.

He cleared his throat. "You okay?"

"Hmm?" She turned to him with a distracted look.

"Back there . . . don't let that get to you."

"That I'm under suspicion for murder? That the police I'm trying to help think I'm some sick killer? Why would I be upset about that?"

The driver's gaze jerked to them in the rear-view mirror, and Darius glared at the man until he returned his attention to the road.

"What do you care what they think? You didn't do it." He slid closer on the seat. "While they're scratching their asses, we'll be closing in on her."

Her mouth twitched and she sent him an amused look. "Scratching their asses?"

Her smile lifted his spirits and made his own mouth curl into a grin.

After a moment her smile melted away. Silence fell again and she went back to looking out the window, every inch of her radiating displeasure. Evidently she couldn't shake her encounter with those idiot detectives. He breathed with relief when the car stopped in front of their hotel. He much preferred talking to her without someone listening in.

They stepped from the car and he quickly paid the driver. The sun was starting to set. He grasped her arm to lead her into the hotel so they could get ready for the party tonight. Their first real lead. He had to look at it that way. It was the only way he could stomach the notion of hanging out at a frat party with a bunch of smashed college students.

She pulled free of him. "I need a little air. Just a short walk."

She started down the sidewalk, and he fell into step beside her.

She stopped and swung to face him, crossing her arms defensively across her chest. "I don't require an escort."

"Well, you have one." He continued on a few steps, stopping when he saw that she wasn't with him. He turned to look back at her.

She stared up at him, cold determination in those cat eyes of hers. And a certain frostiness. "I'm not going to run away. Surely you know—"

"That's not what I'm afraid of." Until the words escaped him, he hadn't realized they were the truth. In his eyes, she wasn't his prisoner anymore. Somehow, in all of this, the scales had tipped and placed them on an equal footing.

He no longer saw her as his opponent. His perspective had changed. *He* had changed.

The elegant twin slashes of her eyebrows drew together. "Then why—"

"Better than anyone, you know how unsafe this world is."

"I've managed this long without you."

"Oh. Is that what you've been doing? Managing?" He shook his head. "What you've been doing is running. Hiding. How many years have you spent secluded, in utter isolation in subarctic climates, eking out an existence?"

A shutter fell over her eyes, but before it did he caught a glimpse of hurt. Ridiculous, of course. How could anything he said wound this witch who had lived a couple thousand years and cursed countless lives to miserable deaths? Nothing should be able to touch her. Especially not him.

He sighed and dragged a hand through his hair. There he went again, reminding himself of what she was. Because apparently he needed that reminder. He needed it to be wrong that he was drawn to her . . . attracted to her.

She stiffened, pulling back her shoulders as though bracing for an attack. "I get by," she whispered.

He snorted. "Sure."

"Just like you," she flung back, fire flashing in her gaze. Before he could respond, before he could say, *You don't know a thing about me,* she turned and stormed away.

He rushed after her, hauling her back to face him. "I *don't* 'get by.' That's why I'm here," he admitted, breathing harshly. "I'm not satisfied with my life. My existence. Are you trying to tell me you are?"

A couple skirted past them on the sidewalk, giving them plenty of room.

Cursing beneath his breath, he pulled her into an alley between the hotel and a coffee shop. She tripped trying to keep up and he caught her, stopping her from falling.

"I don't get by," he repeated, backing her against the brick wall. As he stared down at her, her scent filled his nose. His breath fell in harsh rasps. "And I have you to thank for that."

Her face crumpled. "Don't you think I know that? Don't you think I think of that every day? Every lycan out there is because of me, their hellish existence because of me . . ."

He sucked in a hissing breath. He didn't mean *that*. He was thinking about her effect on him. About the torment of being near her, wanting her, and not being able to have her. Especially now that he knew her scent, her taste . . . her passion. It was all he could do not to pull her to him and take her.

But he couldn't let her know that. He shouldn't.

He hated how his heart clenched at the pain etched into her face. "So that means I should just forget and forgive?"

"I didn't ask that of you." She shook her head. "I wouldn't."

"But it's there. Since I met you, a voice in my head keeps telling me to forgive you."

"Don't," she said simply, shaking her head. "I don't deserve it." Her dark hair swished around her like ink. His hands itched to gather it up.

He looked away, every sense alive and vibrating with an aching awareness of her. Her words echoed inside him. *Don't. I don't deserve it.*

Damn her, she *would* have to say that. Show herself to be humble. The opposite of what she was supposed to be, but precisely the type of female he couldn't resist.

He released a pent-up sigh and faced her again. "It's too late."

She blinked, her eyes enormous with astonishment. As he took a heavy lock of her hair between his fingers, gently rubbing the silky strands, she stilled, freezing like prey in his grasp.

"You're nothing you should be," he whispered.

Her mouth parted on a soft gasp, her expression so damned innocent. So sweetly provocative. It only furthered his frustration. Squeezed a fist around his heart.

Before he could reconsider he acted on every impulse pumping through his blood. He slid his hand around her neck and pulled her mouth to his. Her lips were even more delicious than he remembered. Soft and warm and yielding. Nothing he deserved. Nothing he'd thought possible. Not from her.

His fingers closed around the back of her neck, the silk of her hair grazing his hand. He brought his other hand to her face, cupping her cheek, so soft against his rasping palm.

She tasted of sweetness and life. She was light. Not the death she'd brought to him and so many others.

His hands flexed against her softness, pulling her closer. Her arms wrapped around his waist, drawing him against her, her hands flattening against his back. Heat coursed through him. His skin snapped and pulled, the beast inside him waking, prowling beneath the surface, hungering, needing.

It wasn't enough. He wanted more. Wanted to crawl inside her, fuse himself into her so that these feelings never ended. So he didn't have to go back to the gnawing ache again.

To the void that could never be filled.

He flinched at the prospect, fear nipping his heels. And that shook him even more. That he should feel so panicked at being without *her* shook him.

When had she come to matter so much to him? How had he allowed that to happen?

He tore his hands free and stepped back, horror tripping through him.

She fell against the brick wall as though she couldn't hold herself up without his arms around her. Her chest rose and fell with heavy breaths. She lifted a hand to her lips, her fingers shaking as she traced them. The gold in her eyes shined molten in the burnished air, lighting a fire to him.

"Why d-did you . . ." Her voice faded.

He shook his head, unable to answer. Unwilling.

Turning, he left her, his hands opening and closing at his sides, aching for the feel of her again. He forced his feet to move ahead.

He wasn't worried that she would run away. Wanting this witch captured drove her with a desperate intensity. Just like finding Balthazar and ending his curse drove him. There wasn't room for anything else.

Until he was free of this curse, there never could be.

TRESA WATCHED HIM GO, her mind spinning, her lips burning, her heart pounding.

She touched the hair he had stroked and held. She'd forgotten how gentle a man's hand could be. She choked on a sob and covered her mouth. Who would have thought she could have found that again in the arms of a lycan?

She stood leaning against the wall for several more minutes, until she felt more composed. Even so, she wasn't ready to return to the room and face him.

She turned right, away from the hotel, and continued swiftly down the sidewalk. She passed several storefronts, upscale shops and boutiques that catered to people who lived happy, untarnished lives.

She shivered despite the balmy evening. Twinkly lights in a pet store window blinked cheerfully. She stopped and stared through the glass at the puppies. She'd owned several dogs over the years—dogs that she had loved, whose warmth she'd savored on the cold, long nights. They were her companions, the best thing she could ever hope to have. She couldn't let herself have more. At least that's what she'd always told herself.

How could she have a relationship with another person, given what she was, what she'd done? Even Darius was too good for her.

A puppy stood on its hind legs and pawed the glass. She pressed a palm to the window. A pet was the best she could have. It was the best she could allow herself. Even knowing how impossible Darius's kiss, his touch—*anything* she shared with him was— Remorse filled her. And longing.

Knowing she didn't deserve to ever feel anything remotely *good* was a hard thing to accept when presented with the temptation. And Darius was all temptation.

Everything in her had come alive in his arms. He'd woken that dormant part of her that remembered what it felt like to be loved. She never thought she could feel again anything close to what she'd had with Michel. Now she knew it was possible. *More than possible.*

She inhaled and dropped her hand from the glass. Turning, she headed back to the hotel, her steps slow. She may have discovered it was possible to feel alive again, but it was bittersweet because it was impossible for her to let that happen.

She'd given up the right to feel alive when she'd sold her soul to Balthazar.

FOURTEEN

Darius listened to the sound of Tresa's movements. She'd returned to their room subdued. Avoiding his gaze, she'd gathered a few things and disappeared into the bathroom.

She took a long time in the shower, but he guessed most women did. Strange. He'd never thought of her like that. A woman with normal needs. Someone who took her time getting ready to go out. But now he knew, of course, that she was all too similar to mortal women. With vulnerabilities. Needs. Desires.

Now he couldn't think of her any other way. As a woman with needs that matched his own.

A few years ago, he'd only wanted companionship. To find a mate to help fill the void, the emptiness. Another lycan like himself, who didn't embrace the pack mentality.

He'd given up on that idea, having discovered it wasn't that simple. A life cursed can never be easy and carefree.

Finding someone had been a fanciful notion. A fairy tale. His energies were better invested in trying to break his curse. For himself, his soul . . . for all mankind. As long as he existed like this, he was a danger.

The sound of the hair dryer died away, a sign, he hoped, that she would be out soon. He was eager to get going. He knew these college parties probably started late, but being alone with her in this hotel room wrecked him. At least so soon after that kiss. He could still taste her. His hands could still feel her . . .

Control was something he constantly struggled with, not just at the moonrise. His urges always ran strong. He told himself he just needed a little time to recover from that kiss with Tresa. He'd reclaim his control soon enough; he always did. Then the urge to have her—*take* her—wouldn't burn through him like a maelstrom.

The thought of having her, parting her thighs and sinking himself inside her heat . . . It didn't even disgust him anymore. And without that disgust, what was to keep him at arm's length?

He groped for the once-held belief that she was evil.

He snorted and sank down onto the bed, dragging his hands through his hair. Hell, he didn't believe that anymore. He couldn't. And that was the problem.

He was finding it harder and harder to reconcile the Tresa of lore to the one before him. She honestly seemed to care about stopping this killer . . . stopping Balthazar.

But she had started the curse. All of this. She was responsible for so much misery.

He couldn't forget that. He wouldn't.

The door to the bathroom opened and she stepped out, looking sexy and smelling fresh, her scent heady and intoxicating. He closed his eyes in a pained blink, squeezing his hands into fists at his sides to stop himself from reaching for her.

He opened his eyes and struggled for indifference, cloaking it around himself as his gaze skimmed her slim legs encased in tight black leggings and knee-high heeled boots. She wore a soft-looking snug gray tunic sweater that subtly molded her curves and begged for his hand to caress.

She quickly attached a pair of shimmery earrings to her earlobes. Her gaze flicked to him, and then away. It was the most she had looked at him since she'd returned from her walk. "Ready?" she murmured.

"Yeah." And yet he didn't move. He simply stared at her, his mind whirling with the knowledge that he didn't want to go anywhere. He wanted to stay here—in this room with her. Kissing her again. And again. Stripping that soft-looking sweater off her. Laying her on the bed. Covering her lithe body with his own. His body pulsed with hunger, need pumping through him in a way he had never experienced.

She fidgeted beneath his intent stare and glanced down at herself. "What? Do I look okay?"

He devoured every delicious inch with his eyes before forcing his gaze away. "Yeah," he said roughly. "Not inconspicuous, but . . ."

"Was I supposed to be inconspicuous?" she asked sharply, her eyes glinting defensively. "I thought we wanted people to talk to us?"

He looked her over. "Oh, they'll definitely want to talk to you. At least the guys will. But we're looking for a female."

Faint colored stained her cheeks. "Well. We have you for them, don't we?" She moved for the door with stiff, angry movements. "Let's get this over with."

He followed her, hearing what she wasn't saying. *Let's get this over with so we can end this and never have to see each other again.*

Only he couldn't imagine that happening. Not now that he'd met her. *Liked* her.

He wasn't ready to let her go.

THE HOUSE WAS PACKED to the seams when they arrived. Tresa was sure they were breaking every fire code with the hundred-plus twenty-year-olds crammed inside. Heavy bass pumped in the air, vibrating the floor beneath her feet. Beer sloshed in red plastic cups as they squeezed through the throng.

Darius led the way, one hand clamped tightly around her wrist. She was glad for that. She didn't want to lose him in this throng, and his grip was less intimate than if his fingers were laced with her own.

He moved with purpose, so she assumed he knew where he was going. They stopped in the dining area. The dining table was pushed to the side, along the wall, and littered with giant plastic bowls of chips and pretzels.

Several kegs of beer stood beside the table, surrounded by preppy-looking guys in button-down shirts. They looked Darius over appraisingly, puffing out their chests as if preparing to battle for territory.

"Darius!" a voice screeched over the din.

Erin bounced toward them, beer sloshing over the rim of her cup. "You made it!"

She hugged him, pressing against him breasts that looked dangerously close to spilling free from her slinky, glittery tank top.

Tresa watched them embrace, hands at her sides, acutely uncomfortable. Erin stood on her tiptoes and whispered something in Darius's ear. Heat crawled up Tresa's neck as she stood by in silence, ignored.

The guys guarding the keg eyed her up and down, making her feel like a piece of meat. One said something behind his hand and the others laughed. The heat in her face grew and suddenly she felt intensely claustrophobic. She wasn't accustomed to this. She lived in isolation, her only company howling winds. Her skin tingled with a thousand needle pricks. The faces around her began to blur together. This was a terrible idea.

Erin's gaze locked on Tresa. She gave her a brief nod, her expression superior, confident as she wrapped an arm around Darius's waist. Erin said something and Darius lowered his head to hear her over the din. She took advantage of the opportunity and touched his face, her hands lightly stroking his jaw.

Tresa stomach revolted. Then someone

bumped her roughly as they squeezed past. She had to get out of here.

Turning, she pushed through the press of bodies. Impossible as it seemed, the house was even more crowded now.

"Hey there, Tresa." Carson was suddenly there, grinning in welcome. "Glad you could make it." He spread his arms widely. "*Mi casa es su casa*."

"Hey," Tresa greeted him over the noise, her gaze darting nervously as people continued bumping into her. She stuck out her elbows, trying to make space for herself amid the sea of bodies.

"Where you going?" he called out over the volume.

"I need some air."

She looked around, catching no sight of Darius. Though he was taller than most guys here, she couldn't see him anymore. The image of Erin flashed through her mind. She was probably dragging him into a bedroom upstairs for a quickie. The blood rushed to her face at the sudden image of them together, going at it in a fever of sex.

Maybe that kiss earlier had whetted his appetite and he would slake his unanswered desires on Erin.

"Come on. I'll help you." Carson's hand

closed over hers and soon he was zigzagging them through the crowd.

She kept her head low and followed, glad to know she'd be free of this suffocating press of people soon. In the back of her mind she wondered how she was supposed to gather information about any of the victims when she couldn't even abide being here.

They cleared a set of double doors and stepped out into the mild night. Voices and music throbbed behind her. She moved ahead of Carson, walking several feet out into the yard, craving distance from the jumble of humanity. She stopped beside a large oak, gripping the rough bark as if it were a lifeline.

"You okay?" Carson's hand settled on her back. His face was close, etched in concern.

"Fine." She gulped a clean breath. "I don't do crowds."

He smiled in sympathy. "Then why did you come here?"

"Guess it didn't occur to me that it would be quite this crowded."

He angled his head. "It's a party. More than that, it's Jason Morris's final hurrah. Everyone's got to show up to say farewell to that dickhead." A sneer entered his voice. "Funny how in death you become such a saint."

Her attention focused sharply. "Why was he a dickhead?"

"He was a player. He'd do anything to get into a girl's pants, and then he'd trash-talk her afterward. The guy destroyed lives but it never hurt his rep. Girls kept falling for him."

Like Balthazar's witch? Is that what had happened? Had he used her and cast her aside afterward? It seemed plausible. But what about the female victims? What could they have done to get on her bad side?

"Shannan Guzak and the other girls. Did Jason ever trash-talk them?"

He snorted. "Doubtful. Those were regular hookups. He didn't piss them off. They kept coming back for more. I saw Shannan leave Jason's room the night before she died."

Tresa nodded, processing this. The female victims had all slept with Jason Morris. He was the connection. Maybe one of his hookups had been Balthazar's witch. But if Carson was to be believed, the list of candidates was long.

"Hey." His hand rubbed small circles against her back. "You okay? You're not having one of your visions, are you?" He brushed the hair back from her face and she was suddenly aware of just how alone they were. The party was in full swing in the well-lit house several feet away, but they stood in dark shadows.

She laughed weakly, uncomfortable with his closeness. "No. I'm not."

"So." He ran a finger down her cheek. "My little psychic—can you see the future? Are you and I going to become good friends?"

She stepped clear of his hand, not liking where this was headed. "Look. I need to find Darius."

"Thought you two weren't together."

"We're not."

"Then what's your hurry? He's probably having a good time with Erin." He closed the distance between them again. "And I thought you didn't like it in there, anyway. Why not stay out here with me where it's nice and quiet?" His fingers grazed her face again. "I like talking to you . . . hearing your voice."

She grasped Carson's hand and tried to pull it from her cheek, but he resisted. "I'm sorry if I've given you the wrong kind of idea—"

"How can I be around you and *not* get the wrong kind of idea?" He released a gust of alcohol-laden breath. "You're just so fucking hot." He unexpectedly pressed his mouth over hers in a moist, clumsy kiss. She gagged at the slimy sensation of his tongue pushing inside her mouth.

She shoved against his chest, ready to push him back, but she didn't get the chance.

He was suddenly flying through the air, landing on his back several yards away with a loud grunt. Darius stood there, legs braced wide, chest heaving, as he looked down at Carson. The boy moaned, rolling on his side.

She made a move toward Carson. "Did you hurt him?" She wanted to say, *Did you kill him?*—but caught herself.

Darius grabbed her arm, stopping her. "I hope so," he bit out. "That was the idea."

Her gaze snapped to his livid face. "That wouldn't be a good idea. You. In jail. For murder—not good." She looked back at Carson in concern.

"He's fine," Darius growled.

She twisted her arm free. "Did you have to throw him like that?"

"Hey!" The sound of Carson's voice caught her attention. He rose unsteadily to his feet, limping a pace away, clutching his side. "Back off, man. She said you two weren't together—"

"We're not!" Tresa snapped, turning her glare on Darius.

Darius cocked his head, his pewter eyes glinting sharply in the gloom. "I thought his advances were unwelcome. Should I have left you to enjoy yourself with him?"

She inhaled and flexed her hands at her sides. "It was under control. I was handling it. I don't need you swooping in to rescue me."

He snorted.

She stiffened, still glaring.

"You two crazy fucks deserve each other!" Carson slapped a hand in the air at them and staggered back inside the house.

Squaring her shoulders, she moved past Darius to follow Carson inside, determined to suffer the hot press of bodies again, the girls with their overpowering perfumes and hair products. She'd come here to get information. She'd gotten a little from Carson, enough to know she needed to build a list of all the girls Jason Morris had slept with.

"Where are you going?" Darius growled, falling into step beside her.

"Back inside. We came here to do a job."

"Oh? And do you have to kiss any other college boys to get it done?"

She cut him a scathing glance. He was one to talk. "Why don't you go find Erin? I'm sure she's looking for you."

His expression darkened.

She took the steps up to the door, feeling

Darius behind her. He radiated displeasure. Somehow she didn't think he would stray far from her this time, and she was relieved.

She squeezed through the bodies, pasting a smile on her face. Like it or not, she was going to have to be friendly if she wanted people to talk to her.

Suddenly Erin was there again, bouncing in front of her. "Hey! Have you seen—" Her gaze drifted beyond her shoulder. "Oh! Darius! There you are!"

She shoved past Tresa and planted herself in front of him. His hand slipped from around Tresa's. Annoyed, Tresa plunged ahead, squeezing through bodies and sloshing cups. He could play with Erin all he liked. She had work to do.

Still, she stole a glance behind her. Erin was plastered to Darius, talking into his ear. He stared down at her, a vaguely perplexed expression on his face, as if he didn't know quite how to disengage from this female.

"Hey there!" A guy reeking of marijuana and beer tossed an arm over her shoulder. She staggered beneath the weight. "You looking *good,* baby."

"Um, hey," she greeted him, suspecting that in his current condition, he wasn't going to be the most useful source of information.

"Can I get you a beer?" he slurred.

She opened her mouth to accept his offer, hoping that he'd leave her to fetch that drink, and then she stopped, a hot wash of fear twisting inside her. A terror that she hadn't felt in over a year, but knew so well.

She scanned the crowd, her veins burning cold, and a gasp escaped her when she saw the writhing black shape amid the bodies, winding toward her like a serpent.

Balthazar.

He'd found her.

FIFTEEN

She had no doubt he'd known the moment she arrived in town. Now, for whatever reason, he'd finally decided to reveal himself. She knew that by coming here she was taking a chance, but she'd hoped he'd leave her alone.

Panicked, she began pushing through the crowd, clawing with her hands, using her elbows, heedless of whom she might hurt. She didn't look back, the old memories of all those times he'd possessed her too terrifying.

She knew it was inevitable. She couldn't outrun him. He'd found her. He would claim her. Still, she couldn't docilely accept it.

She choked on a sob, regretting coming. Regretting what was about to happen to her. Hopefully she could be free of this house and all these people before he possessed her. God knew what evil he'd force her to do here, with all these innocents.

Desperate little cries spilled from her lips.

She tripped out the back door, landing flat on her face. Hands bleeding from the impact, she picked herself up and raced into the trees as fast as she could. Her feet pounded over the brittle, dry grass. Wind lashed at her cheeks, chilling the wetness on her skin as salty tears rolled down her face.

Leaves rustled around her, and she knew it was him. Closing in. She felt the heat of him at her back, nipping her heels. He was on her. No sense in running another step.

Sucking in a deep breath, she spun and faced him, bracing herself to fight him like every time before. And like every time before, she hoped this time would be different. That she could somehow hold him off. She prayed for a miracle.

She glimpsed his dark shape before she was swept up in the spinning storm of him, her feet coming off the ground. She dangled, airborne. Dark air circled her like a cyclone, roaring in her ears. And then she was lost. Thrust into a dark corner inside herself.

She was his.

DARIUS UNWRAPPED ERIN'S ARMS from his neck, ignoring her protests, his gaze fastened on Tresa as she fled the house, her movements as panicked and desperate as a hare pursued by hounds. Something was wrong.

Terror gleamed in her eyes and his skin tightened, snapping with awareness. He'd never seen her like this. Even when he'd shown up at her house and manhandled her, she hadn't shown such fear.

He looked behind her, trying to identify the source of her panic. Nothing. No one pursued her. People cried out complaints as she barreled past them, shoving rudely in her escape.

She dove out the back door and he cut through the crowd after her. When he stepped outside, she was a small figure racing through the woods behind the house, well past the point where he had discovered her with Carson earlier.

He called her name, but she didn't stop. It was like she couldn't even hear him.

Sudden realization struck him. *What was the one thing that could strike terror in her heart?*

With a curse, he quickened his pace, moving at blurring speed, catching up to her easily. Only, she had stopped. Stood, with an eerie stillness, amid the trees.

He paused. Even without seeing her face he

could tell there was something different. Something off. She didn't hold herself with her usual guardedness. There was a relaxed air about her. He'd never seen her like this, all loose limbed . . . her guard dropped so completely.

"Tre?" The name slipped out, felt natural. Especially in this moment when he was concerned about her. He walked around her, scanning her from head to toe.

She didn't appear injured. She was hardly even out of breath from her sprint through the woods. She was as still as a statue but her gaze fastened on him with the avidness of a hawk. She looked different . . . and yet the same. He couldn't pinpoint what was different, but everything about her was wrong.

"Tre?" he whispered.

"She's not here." The voice belonged to Tresa but it wasn't her. Not at all.

It was the final confirmation of the sick premonition churning inside him. This wasn't her. It was Balthazar.

Then he saw her eyes. The lovely whiskey brown was gone, replaced with a tar black that gleamed like spilled oil.

Her nostrils flared like those of a beast scenting the air. "What have we here? A lycan? How . . . singular."

"Balthazar?" he demanded.

"Ah. You know my name. I'm afraid you have me at a disadvantage, then, because I don't know yours. Come now. Don't be rude. Introduce yourself."

"Darius."

"Darius." The demon-possessed Tresa began to circle him slowly, assessing him. "A lycan not like any other lycan I've ever seen. You don't stink of death." She lifted her face up and sniffed the air. "You don't feed. How unique." She stopped and propped a hand on her hip. "How is it that you've come to be in the company of my sweet Tresa? She is sweet, isn't she . . . my little minx? Even if she isn't cooperative." She smiled, her lips stretching widely. "I am fond of the girl even if she has been a thorn in my side for so many years. What can I say?" She shrugged. "We love our children no matter what."

He felt a growl rumble up from his throat and resisted the urge to bite out that Tresa didn't belong to this demon. Especially since she in fact did. The proof of that was before him now in those tar black eyes and cruelly smiling lips.

"Where is she?" he demanded.

Tresa's arms spread wide. "Here, of course.

Look no further." Her face, with its curling lips and devious expression, made her look like an entirely different female. She looked evil. This was what he'd expected when he went looking for her.

"Did you wish to say something to her? Go ahead . . . she can hear you. Well, probably. She's being very difficult right now, trying to reject me. She's such a naughty one. Always going against me." Despite her jovial tone, a hardness glittered in those eyes. Balthazar wasn't pleased with her.

"Let her go. You have another more willing medium these days."

"That I do, that I do. A most accommodating host. *She* doesn't fight me. I don't even have to guide her. Leaving her to her own devices has been—" Tresa suddenly looked like she was savoring the finest chocolate. "Gratifying. She's most creative. I've enjoyed giving her free rein. I can't wait to see what she does next." Tresa motioned at herself in disgust. "Unlike Tresa. She's useless to me."

Darius gestured back toward the house. "Is she here? Your new witch? Who is she?"

Tresa's mouth curled wickedly and she crossed her arms over her chest in gratification. "Wouldn't you like to know."

Suddenly Tresa cringed and bent over, clutching her middle.

Darius moved in her direction, his instinct to help. Until he recalled that this wasn't Tresa. Not anymore. He stopped and forced his hands to his sides.

She flipped her head back up, tossing her dark hair and glaring at him. Soulless eyes gleamed out like death at him. "She's especially fierce tonight. Might that have something to do with you, dog?"

"Let her go," he commanded. "Come out and fight me yourself."

A laugh rippled from her lips, alien and sinister. "You think you can defeat me? You can't even see me. I'm only a shadow to your eyes."

"I'll take my chances."

"Hmm. You could just kill her." She made a slicing motion to her throat. "Cut off Tresa's head and I'll be free . . . and I'll form right before your eyes. We could have it out in true style. You could kill me then."

Darius's hands grew damp, his stomach knotting at the thought. He couldn't do such a thing. Even if it was the only way he could see Balthazar.

Even if Darius could see him, he'd be hard to kill. Every demon possessed an Achilles' heel, his mark of the fall. This mark could be any-where on the demon's body. He'd have to find it first and then strike there, *only* there. Not an easy task when the demon was a mere shadow.

Tresa's demon continued talking. Even in Tresa's voice, it didn't sound like her. It sounded evil. Strange that he had thought her that very thing. But she wasn't evil. This thing in front of him was.

"You don't actually care about her, do you? This witch that started your curse?" Black eyes looked him over, considering him, *seeing* him. "Clearly you don't wish to be what you are. I can see that. How can you care about *her* life?" With a tsking sound, Balthazar nodded. "She deserves to be punished . . . her life ended. You know it's true."

Rage swelled up inside Darius. A week ago he would have agreed without hesitation. Rather than explain his change of heart to this demon, he taunted him with a beckoning wave of his hand. "Shadow or no, let's have a go-round."

Tresa suddenly released a hissing breath, bending at the waist as though in pain. The black of her eyes shuddered, the whites appear-ing for a second before vanishing, plunging to black again.

"Tre?" he called, knowing instantly she was in there, fighting to return.

"Bitch," Balthazar growled in a contorted, garbled voice, "can you never just stay put and do what you're commanded to do?"

With an unnatural howl, a great gust of wind surged free from her body, the air murky with the demon's vague shape.

The inky shadow whirled around Darius, taunting him. Leaves and dirt blew, nearly blinding him. He lurched forward and caught Tresa up in his arms just as she collapsed. Her arms loosely circled his shoulders.

"Sorry," she said hoarsely in his ear. "So . . . sorry . . ."

He squinted at the cloudy shape circling them both, trying to discern the demon within.

A voice came from the clouded figure, scratching the air like sandpaper on his flesh. "You can't destroy me, lycan!"

And then he was gone, a dark plume winding back toward the house.

"She's in there." Tresa struggled to stand on her own, pointing toward the distant house. "He's returning to her." Her words rushed with urgency. "We have to go find her. Now! It's our chance."

She took a stumbling step toward the house.

She didn't make it a second step before her knees buckled. He gathered her close. Her heart beat like a drum against her chest. He could feel every thud. He pushed back the dark hair from her face. "How are we going to do that when you can't even walk?"

"Sorry," she panted, her gaze fixed on the house. "I'm always weak . . . after . . . It was harder to fight him here. Without the cold, he's stronger." Her eyes drifted shut and she went limp in his arms.

For a moment an irrational fear seized his heart. He jostled her in his arms. "Tre!" Relief filled him when she moaned. She was okay. Just drained. He lifted her, holding her close like she was something fragile. Which was ironic, considering that she was the least fragile creature he'd ever met. The woman hadn't survived for generations by being weak.

Holding her in his arms, he circled back to the front of the house, finding his car parked alongside the road with dozens of other vehicles. He secured her carefully in the passenger seat, buckling her in. Her head drooped to the side and silky dark hair fell into her face. He smoothed the hair back, tucking a lock behind her ear. She looked so young and innocent. Not at all like a woman who had lived over two thousand years.

With a sigh, he closed the door. For a moment he hesitated, his gaze drifting to the house. Light and noise spilled out on to the street. Balthazar was in there. And his witch. She was probably closing in on her next victim, Balthazar egging her on.

Shaking his head, he climbed behind the wheel. He couldn't possibly leave Tresa in the car and resume hunting the witch. Not in this condition.

Reaching across the seat he brushed the backs of his fingers against the gentle curve of her cheek. It seemed he couldn't stop himself from touching her. He needed to feel her, needed to assure himself that she was all right. Strong and well. Somehow that had become his priority.

She needed him right now. And he wouldn't let her down.

SIXTEEN

Tresa woke to a dark room.

She sat up with a gasp, fighting and kicking against the covers, her mind and body reliving the sensation of being trapped inside herself. Balthazar controlling her, taking over until she was locked up in that dark corner of her mind again and unable to do anything. Unable to stop him. It was horrible, second only to the terror she'd felt when she was drowning, water filling her, burning up her lungs . . . consuming her.

Tears clogged her throat, running hotly down her cheeks as she thrashed, struggling to break free.

"Tre! Tre!" Hands grasped her arms and she struck out blindly, her knuckles making contact with hard, unyielding muscle.

"Tre. It's me, Darius. You're safe."

She stilled, the words sinking in. *Darius.*

She went weak, her body trembling. She

pushed back the hair from her face, hating how her fingers shook.

She was safe. With a lycan. That irony tightened her throat. But as his hands closed around her arms, it felt *right*. Too right.

Her encounter with Balthazar had shaken her to her core. These past months had been so peaceful without him. She'd forgotten just how terrible it was when he possessed her and she lost control of herself. Tonight had brought that all back to her.

And Darius had been there to witness her shame. Perhaps that stung the most.

She swallowed. "I'm sorry. I should have been stronger—"

"To fight off a possession? It's harder in warm temperatures, right?" He was a shadowy outline on the bed, but she perceived his shaking head. "You did all you could. And you did reclaim yourself eventually."

She looked down, nodding mutely, uncomfortable with the idea of him making excuses for her. Compassion . . . understanding. She didn't deserve it from him.

He smoothed the hair that veiled her face. The tenderness of the gesture shook her.

"Tell me," he softly commanded. "I want to understand."

She lifted her gaze. Even in the gloom, his pewter eyes shimmered.

"What?" she whispered, even though she already sensed it. He wanted to know everything. He was ready to hear about her past. To find out *why* everything had happened. Why she'd surrendered to Balthazar. To *know* her. He wanted to understand. Even though he shouldn't, even though she shouldn't accept this from him . . .

Silence floated between them. There was a rustle of movement and then a click as he turned on the bedside lamp. She blinked at the dull glow flooding the room. The muted light softened his features. He looked less harsh, the hard angles less severe. No resemblance to the hard-faced lycan who'd first shown up in her house.

He sat on the edge of the bed, his hands gliding down her arms to her hands. His broad palms lightly covered her fingers. The heat of his skin radiated over her, warming her from the inside out.

"How have you survived for so long?" he asked.

"I can't die." She twisted one shoulder in a weak shrug. "I don't have a choice."

"There were choices. You didn't end up in

some padded room. And you didn't turn out like this other witch, either, relishing hurting others, embracing evil."

She wet her lips and his eyes followed the movement. Her stomach tightened. Everything inside her told her to look away, to slide her hands out from under his and scoot a little farther down the bed.

"I just wanted Etienne Marshan punished . . . I watched him kill my husband, my grandmother. They were the only family I had. And then Balthazar came, promising to punish Etienne."

Bleakness consumed her as she stared at him, remembering the old hurt. "I never wanted this to happen. I didn't think he would do anything to hurt anyone else. Just Etienne. God, every day since, I've wished I'd died with Michel and Grandmère. If I had just drowned . . ."

She dragged her hands free and pulled her knees to her chest, burying her face between them. The misery that was never very far washed over her.

A strong, warm hand claimed hers, covering it completely. He made tender shushing sounds, so at odds with what she expected from him. What she deserved.

Shaking her head, she pulled her hand away.

"No. Don't treat me like I'm something to be pitied." She started to rise but he pulled her back, folded her in his arms.

She reacted, struggling. He pinned her with his body, his hands coming up to frame her face, and she stilled, captured by his gaze.

The sensation of his hands on her face, the raspy palms against her cheeks, pulled at everything inside her, and she felt something deep within her unraveling, like a ribbon on a package coming loose.

"What are you doing?" She simply breathed the words, her eyes on his mouth, recalling with desperate hunger the taste of him. Her chest tightened, her lungs constricting with the fear, the hope, the prayer, right or wrong, that he would kiss her again.

He shook his head once, as though jogging some sense into himself. With a ragged breath, he released her and sat back. His shoulders rose and fell as he lowered his head into his hands, seizing fistfuls of the dark hair. "I don't know anything anymore."

His voice sounded pained, regretful—as if he couldn't stand himself for touching her so intimately. Of course. However horrible he was, she was worse.

She scooted down the bed, her heart heavy.

"I'm sorry," she muttered. Helplessly. Inanely. It was all she could say. "You shouldn't touch me. You shouldn't even be here."

Ridiculously hurt that he wasn't disagreeing with her, she reached the end of the bed, dropping her legs over until her feet touched the ground.

The hurt was there. A deep pang in her chest. She glanced over her shoulder at him. He clasped his head in his hands as if he was weary.

She lowered her shaking hands on the edge of the mattress and pushed up. She wasn't quite standing yet when his hand clamped on her wrist, his strong fingers a warm vise. She hadn't even heard him move.

He pulled her around to face him in one smooth move. She stared at him in surprise.

"I've never done anything I should," he told her. One hand dove into her hair and cupped the back of her head as his lips met hers.

He fell back on the bed, taking her with him. She sprawled over him, her lower body slipping between his thighs. His lips moved passionately on hers, loving hers, devouring her.

He kissed her like he was starved for her. Like this was his last kiss on the last day of his life. She touched his cheeks, caressing his face, assuring herself that this moment was real and not some dream.

The dark mass of her hair fell around them in a veil, and his fingers gathered all the strands, holding them back.

Her excitement increased, as did the kiss. He might have started it, but now she was fully invested. Desire hummed and sparked through every nerve. She felt alive as she hadn't since the day she'd died.

She angled her head to deepen the kiss, desperate to get closer, to fuse them together. She pressed herself against him, moving and thrusting her hips with an instinct that was deep and strong.

With Darius she didn't have to think. There was just sensation. Just *this*.

His arms circled her waist and he flipped her on her back, coming over her with every tasty inch of him. Her hands roamed his back and chest, hating the shirt that kept her from feeling his skin against her palms. Her fingers flew to the hem, grasping the fabric and tugging it up. His mouth broke from hers so that she could send the shirt flying.

His lips dragged down her throat, his teeth scraping along her skin in the most delicious way. He growled when he came to the neckline of her sweater and she arched her back so he could pull it free. She didn't even feel the air before he was on her, covering her again. He brought his head down to nuzzle at her black-lace-covered breasts.

She sighed and arched, weaving her fingers through his hair, clutching him close.

His mouth came back to hers. Their lips clung, drinking, tasting, devouring as his hands delved inside her bra, pushing the flimsy fabric aside to expose her sensitive flesh. She gasped into his mouth as he cupped a breast, his palm abrading the aroused nipple.

With a growl, he wrenched his lips from hers, dragging his mouth down the column of her neck, sucking, nipping at the cords of her throat. She heard the thin fabric of her bra tear, but didn't care. She needed his hands fully on her, skin to skin.

Her head dropped back on the bed, a cry rising up in her throat as he clasped her breasts. Her head lolled from side to side, a hoarse plea on her lips.

His rough palms chafed her tender skin. He took her nipples between his thumb and fore-finger and rolled the peaks. She arched her spine, closing her eyes as shards of pleasure-pain spiked through her.

His breath fired against her throat. She opened her eyes to a gleaming silver that consumed her.

He pulled back slightly, holding her gaze for another moment before dipping his head and taking her breast with his mouth. His tongue laved her nipple and then sucked deeply. Moisture rushed between her legs. She begged, her words broken and gravelly, the voice unrecognizable.

He lowered himself down her body, kissing a burning trail as he went. His hands grasped her waistband and in one quick move her leggings were gone. Air caressed her bare skin. And then she felt his hands at her ankles, her calves. Up they slid, skimming the outside of her thighs.

He came over her again, his fingers teasing the inside of her thighs until she instinctively parted her legs wider.

"That's it," he murmured, his hands slipping higher. One finger eased inside her until she nearly wept from pent-up desire. All the way, he never took his eyes off her. They singed her, molten silver so bright, so deep, she was lost in them.

He used his thumb, unerringly finding that most aching, sensitive spot, rolling his finger over it until her knees gave out. He caught her legs then, wrapping them around his hips. She had barely recovered her breath when he was there, large and insistent, sliding inside her.

Their gazes still locked, he paused, the hard length of him throbbing inside her, not fully lodged yet. He held himself still. His shoulders tensed beneath her hands, restraint humming through the corded muscles under her palms. She pulsed, burned, ached, clenching around him, trying to draw him in deeper.

"Please," she choked out, her voice that of some wanton creature who dared to let passion rule her. "*Please.*"

Surrender flashed in his silver eyes, and she felt its echo answer deep inside her.

He finally moved, shattering everything she thought she knew about herself, about him, in a single thrust.

He was buried deep, their bodies joined, fused hotly. He filled her in a way that was more than physical. More than the life she had known these long, long years.

He groaned, the sound reverberating into her. With one hand beneath her and the other gripping her thigh, he moved forcefully, masterfully, stroking in and out of her. Strong fingers dug into her thigh, angling her for deeper penetration, for pleasure so intense it bordered on pain.

The incredible friction drove her mad. She writhed between his hard body and the bed, desperate, searching for something she didn't know, something elusive, something that seemed both near and far away.

"That's it. Let go," he breathed in her ear, taking the lobe between his teeth and biting down hard, sending a bolt of hot sensation bursting through her.

The ache that had started the moment they came together increased, tightening every nerve in her body until she nearly snapped. His thrusts grew harder, faster, until—at last—she exploded into pieces.

She fell, limp, in his arms, shivering like a leaf falling down to earth. He shuddered against her before collapsing. She reveled in the weight of him, his strong body draped over her.

Her cheek rested against one broad shoulder, his skin like steel beneath satin. She inhaled the warm, musky scent of his body, savoring him.

He didn't budge. And she didn't want him to. He pulsed within her, just the barest movement. She remained contentedly pinned between him and the bed for several moments, until he stirred.

He finally rolled over and settled beside her.

She didn't move, afraid that the smallest action would shatter all of this. That with the merest blink she'd wake all alone, the same lost soul as always.

Cool air crawled over her and she shivered, longing for him to come back to her and cover her with the warm press of his body. Another chill chased over her skin, puckering her nipples, and suddenly Darius was there, pulling the covers up over her.

She snuggled deeper into the covers, content that she didn't have to move . . . that she didn't have to say anything, didn't have to put into words what this meant to her.

Everything.

She chased the word away, refusing to let herself think such a dangerous thought.

Darius moved closer, aligning his body with hers. "Get some rest." His arm slid around her waist. After a few moments, she rested her hand on his arm, relishing the solid feel of him, wishing she could have this always.

THE KNIFE'S AN EXTENSION of you. It fits your hand so perfectly. Like it's always belonged there.

The boy beneath you is such a child. No

Jason. Staring down at him, you're almost sorry Jason is gone. This one was such an easy conquest. He'd followed you upstairs unquestioningly—such an eager little puppy.

Carson moans, mewling like a baby through his gag as you dig the point against his cheek. Blood wells up, pooling around the blade's tip. Satisfaction consumes you. Carson's eyes bulge as you dig through your bag and take out a small plastic Ziploc full of rose petals.

He doesn't deserve the petals, but why break with tradition? You take care as you spread the delicate pink blossoms over his torso and arrange them around him on his rumpled, unmade bed. College boys are such slobs.

The party throbs all around you. A frown pulls at your lips. A distraction you don't like. It makes you feel rushed, clumsy in your efforts.

You smear the blade in his blood, streaking it across his face in a splash of red, coating the gleaming surface until it glistens wetly. You drag the knife down the center of his chest.

Carson thrashes wildly. Ignoring his useless efforts, you focus on your task . . . art, really.

Carefully, you readjust the grip in both hands, positioning the knife above his belly, every inch of you quivering with anticipation, waiting for the relief of it to ease into you. Like the last time. And the time before that.

Inhaling, you plunge.

SEVENTEEN

Tresa lurched awake with a choking cry, her hands clutching her belly as though she felt the knife lodged there.

Darius sat up beside her, his hand dropping to her shoulder, squeezing gently. "What is it? What's wrong? Is it her again?"

She swallowed, fighting for breath, and nodded. "She did it again. Carson. She killed Carson."

Darius's eyes gleamed down at her, the silver cutting through the darkness. "The boy from tonight? Erin's cousin?"

She nodded. She should never have left the party. She knew the killer had been there. She'd been with Carson. The witch had probably even seen them together.

And now he was dead.

"It just happened." She shook her head, correcting herself. "It's happening now. They're probably still at the house. I could hear the party in the background. She had him in a room . . . on a bed." She closed her eyes in an agonized blink. She was carving him up on a bed just like the others. Except she was getting bolder. She was killing smack in the middle of a party.

Darius sat up and flipped on the lamp. Light flooded the room. He moved swiftly, dressing himself. She dropped to the floor and found her clothes.

"We're too late. Again," she muttered, holding her sweater tightly to her chest. "Carson's dead."

"Yeah. But maybe she's still there. And maybe you can identify her."

She nodded numbly, dressing quickly. Hard to believe an hour ago she'd been in Darius's arms, reveling in pleasure, feeling things she hadn't felt since Etienne Marshan and Balthazar came and stole everything from her.

The reminder of how she'd spent the evening made her feel guilty. She should have been hunting a demon instead of enjoying herself.

"Tre?" Darius stood at the door, one hand on the doorknob, watching her with a penetrating stare. "You okay?"

No. She wasn't okay. She was afraid of facing Balthazar again. Afraid of what she'd felt wrapped up in Darius. And then ashamed for feeling that way. Too ashamed to admit it to him.

He dropped his hand from the doorknob and faced her, his expression concerned. Her heart squeezed a little, hoping that what they'd shared meant something. That it was more than just a physical release. More than two bodies coming together in need. "Can you do this?"

She blinked. He was asking her? As though she had a choice? The freedom to choose hadn't been hers in fifty lifetimes.

She moved to the door, striding past him. "Of course. Hopefully she's still there and we can single her out."

As they moved down the hall to the elevator, images of Carson's last moments played over and over in her head. She had to have seen or felt something in that brief time she'd been in the witch's head. An action, a whisper of a thought, that gave away some clue to her identity.

As they drove across town back to the frat house, she bit her lip, worrying the tender flesh. Seized with a sudden thought, she dug out Detective Flannery's card and punched her numbers into the phone.

The detective picked up on the first ring. "Was wondering when you would call me."

"I know you don't believe me," she said without preamble.

Darius slid her a long look as he drove.

She continued, "But there's been another murder. At the frat house in the middle of campus. A guy named Carson."

"How do you know this?" Flannery's usually composed voice came across as testy.

"Do you really want an explanation you're not willing to believe, Detective? Go to the house. The killer is probably still there. In the house . . . at the party. Search and question everyone. She's bound to have blood somewhere on her person." Tresa punched end and tossed the phone down.

She shot a quick glance at Darius. A small smile played about his lips.

"What?"

"I like it when you show your fangs."

She snorted. "I didn't think you liked it so much when we first met."

"Yeah . . . well. I was the recipient then."

She stared out at the dark night, wishing they were already there yet dreading what awaited them. "You think they'll come?"

"The cops? Most definitely. Their number

one suspect just called and told them where to find another body. They'll be there in force."

She huffed out a breath as he turned off the highway. "That's right. They were one step from arresting me today." Was that just today? Seemed like days had passed since then. She shook her head and watched as commercial buildings faded into a familiar residential area. They were almost there.

It was past one, but the party was still in full swing as they turned onto the street and jockeyed for a parking place. Possibly even more cars crowded the street.

They found a distant spot and advanced down the street together, quiet and grim, their strides swift. When they entered the front door, Darius took her hand, his grip tight.

"Stay close," he instructed, clearly determined not to lose her again in the crowd.

She nodded, and took the lead, moving up the crowded stairs, her feet pounding on the steps, intent on finding Carson. They opened door after door, earning several shouts from couples making out. At one room, the door was locked. She smoothed a palm over the wood, and she simply knew. She looked at Darius, dread sinking inside her as she nodded.

Darius moved her aside and kicked in the door.

She peered inside. Bile rose up in her throat. Carson was there. Just as she knew he would be.

Just as she had seen him.

Only he wasn't thrashing and fighting for his life against his gag and bindings. He was still, motionless. A bloody, gory mess. So much blood. The smiling, flirting boy was nowhere in evidence.

She looked away, her hand tightening around Darius's.

With a sharp curse, he pulled her out of the room before anyone else could see inside. He glanced up and down the corridor. A drunken couple stumbled out of a room and laughingly descended the stairs.

"I doubt she's still here," Darius said. "There's most likely blood on her. She probably slipped away before anyone looked too closely at her."

"No." She shook her head and lifted her face. "Balthazar is close . . ."

So she was, too.

Downstairs the music was suddenly cut off. Voices rose in protest.

"Everyone, downstairs!" a commanding voice shouted. "Party's over! Outside."

"That was quick." Darius took her hand and led her to the stairs with all the rest streaming from the bedrooms. They filed down the steps as several officers rushed up and past them, including Simpson. He scowled at her as he passed.

Flannery stood at the base of the stairs. Her expression darkened, her lips pulling thin when Tresa's gaze landed on them.

She pointed a finger at Tresa and spoke to a uniformed policeman next to her. Tresa knew what was coming next.

Reaching the base of the steps, she turned to face Darius. "Don't put up a fight."

His eyebrows knit together. "What are—"

Two uniformed officers appeared on either side of Tresa, cutting him off. "Come with me, please? The detective would like a word."

Darius tensed, his arm lashing out, his hand clamping down on her arm, stopping her from going anywhere with them.

"Sir, remove your hand," one of the officers demanded, his hand moving to his holster.

A tremor vibrated through Darius and into her. From the glint in his eyes, she knew he wasn't frightened. And he wasn't about to back down.

She placed her hand over his. "Darius, it's all right. I'll go with them. I didn't do anything wrong. Just wait for me outside."

He looked squarely into her eyes. "I don't see why I can't go, too."

"I'm the one who saw . . . *it* happen. I'll tell them the truth."

"Like before." He shot an annoyed look at the officers who were listening. Clearly, he didn't think the truth would get them anywhere.

"It's fine," she repeated, her gaze searching his face, communicating to him that it was all they could do. Right now, anyway.

Just then, Erin popped up beside Darius, a friend hugged close to her side. Erin shrugged out of her friend's comforting arm and latched onto Darius.

"Oh God, Darius! I'm so glad you're here. Everyone's saying something happened to Carson!" She grabbed his shirtfront, wrinkling it beyond help.

Tresa was swept along then, a policeman on each side of her. She looked over her shoulder at Darius. Even with Erin draped around him, his gaze was fixed on her. There was some comfort in that at least.

"Ms. Morgan." Detective Flannery looked as disapproving as ever as she surveyed Tresa.

"Detective," Tresa greeted her. Looking beyond her shoulder to the swarm of other officers, she said evenly, "You got here quickly."

"Thanks for calling." Flannery studied her intently. It was impossible to tell if she was sincere or not. "You always seem to be in the thick of things." The implication was there. "Do you have anything else you'd like to share?"

"Just that we're too late. Again."

"No one's leaving. We're questioning everyone before releasing them. And then we're getting their names." Flannery considered her for a long moment, her eyes shrewd and assessing. "Why don't you stay beside me as I question everyone?"

Tresa blinked. "What for? You believe me?"

"I believe you have an uncanny ability to turn up at each of these murders." She angled her head thoughtfully. "That you know things you could only know if you were a witness to the crime itself."

Tresa released a breath. Essentially, that's what she was. A witness.

"And I know you didn't kill this boy," Flannery added.

"How do you know that?"

"I've had a car tailing you all night. You've been back at your hotel for the last three hours." She almost smiled. It was the first sign of emotion she'd seen from the detective, and a reminder that she was relatively young and attractive.

Tresa nodded. "You're more thorough than I gave you credit for."

Now there was no mistaking the smile. "If you truly want to help, this is your chance." Flannery motioned for her to follow, her long legs carrying her out the door to where several patrol cars idled. "Come on. We need to secure and process everything inside the house. We'll be conducting interviews outside."

Tresa followed. Outside, she noticed Darius standing with Erin and her friend in a group of drunk twenty-year-olds. Several officers monitored the group, making sure no one slipped away without first being interviewed.

Darius's gaze met hers. She sent him a nod and a smile, trying to reassure him that she wasn't about to be dragged to jail.

His shoulders eased and something lightened in his expression. Something that made her think about the last few hours they'd spent together. Hours that had made her feel almost normal. Normal. And kind of wonderful.

"Ms. Morgan. This way."

She snapped her attention away from Darius and moved on.

EIGHTEEN

Darius? Are you listening to me?"

Darius pulled his attention from where Tresa stood, across a yard swarming with police and crime scene personnel, and looked down at the girl clinging to his arm.

Part of him wanted to shake her off, but she had just lost her cousin tonight. She deserved some sympathy. And anyway, there was nothing else for him to do while Tresa was occupied with the police. Nothing except continue to keep up his guard and see if any of these girls looked suspicious.

Erin's face was splotchy pink from tears. She looked like a child, most of her makeup washed clean. "Where did you go earlier? I was looking for you."

"Tresa and I had something to do—"

"Tresa." She frowned and muttered, "I thought you two weren't a thing. You're joined at the hip."

He opened his mouth to deny there was anything at all between them, but then realized he didn't want to say that anymore. He wouldn't mean it if he did. Staring at Erin, he wasn't sure why he should want to deny his relationship with Tresa to this girl he barely knew.

Erin's friend looked from Darius to where Tresa stood in the distance and snorted. "Like they're not together? Seriously. I don't think so."

Erin glared at her. "No. They're not, Jackie." She looked back at Darius then, but there was less confidence in her gaze. "Right?"

Darius didn't have a chance to reply. Just then they carried the body out. A discernable surge of emotion swept over the crowd as they saw the corpse, hidden from sight inside the coroner's bag. Several of the girls started crying. A few of the guys yelled and shouted profanities at the police, strongly worded suggestions that they find the motherfucker.

"Oh my God! Carson!" Erin buried her face against Darius's chest, wetting his shirtfront with her tears. Her entire body shook with sobs. She lifted her head and screamed out into the crowd, "What kind of fucking animal would do this?"

Jackie patted her back and made shushing

sounds. "Let it out. Let it out." It didn't ease her. Erin only grew more upset.

"Coward! Coward! Show yourself, you bastard!"

There was a surge in the crowd, outrage that was palpable. Everyone moved, shouting, clutching each other or motioning angrily. Someone threw a beer bottle at a cop car.

Darius scanned the crowd, looking for anything or anyone out of the ordinary.

His attention halted on one female. Dressed in black cargo pants, she wore a bulky black sweater that hung loosely on her torso. Swallowed by her ill-fitting clothes, she stood with her arms crossed in front of her.

She didn't move, stood glaring across the yard at Erin, holding herself still, rigid and unaffected by all the furious mourners around her. If looks could kill, Erin wouldn't be faring too well.

Darius studied her. Did she wear another shirt under that bulky sweater? One that was possibly covered in blood?

He nudged Erin's friend. "Who's that?"

Jackie followed his nod. "Oh, that freak? Megan Johnson. Surprised she's even here. This isn't really her scene."

"Yeah? Why?"

The girl leaned in, apparently eager to impart any gossip. "Well, a few months ago she said a guy raped her at a party here." She shrugged as if it was of no consequence.

Darius studied Megan Johnson, whose hatred for Erin was a living, breathing thing. He couldn't detect whether her eyes were demon black across the distance. But that didn't necessarily mean anything; Balthazar could be absent at this particular time.

She was the only one here not focused on the crime—she was focused on the one person who'd yelled insults at the killer. Was Megan who they were after? And had Erin set her off?

His hand tightened on Erin's arm. "Stay close to me," he warned.

She hiccupped and looked up at him, her tearful eyes worshipful. "O-okay."

If Erin had just put herself in danger, he wasn't leaving her alone until he and Tresa managed to get the witch behind bars. He wasn't going to let Balthazar's witch kill someone else. Suddenly, he realized fully that Tresa's mission was his.

"Come with me." He pulled Erin along and cut through all the students waiting their turns to talk to the detectives. Jackie followed them.

An officer stepped in their path, holding up one hand. "What's the prob—"

"We have information."

"W-we do?" Erin looked surprised.

With a curt nod, the officer led them to where Flannery talked to a couple of kids who didn't look sober enough to stand, much less wield a knife.

He went directly to Tresa's side and pulled her away from the interview she was observing. "I think I know who she is."

Flannery appeared at his side, overhearing his announcement. "You psychic, too, now?"

He jerked his head in the direction of Megan Johnson. "I think she needs to move up to the front of the line. When Erin started cursing the killer, that girl looked like she was going to come unglued."

Flannery glanced at Erin and Jackie, sizing them up. Erin nodded, her eyes wide and solemn. Flannery moved off to talk to a couple of officers.

Darius touched Tresa's arm. "You okay?"

She nodded and drew in a deep breath. "She's here. I can sense that much. Balthazar . . . he's close, too."

His gaze moved back to Megan.

"You think it's her?" she asked, following his gaze.

Megan Johnson jerked her arm away as an officer tried to guide her forward. He tried to take hold of her again and she started yelling, "Take your hands off me, you pig!"

At this, the cop dropped all niceties. He seized her arm and dragged her closer. When she fell, he just hauled her back to her feet.

Her wild gaze flew to Erin as she passed. "You bitch!" she shouted, lunging for her.

Erin shrank back against Darius. "She's crazy."

Several officers restrained her and dragged her to a police car.

Flannery reappeared, her expression grim but her eyes shining with the thrill of having found a viable suspect.

Erin looked up at Darius with her large, shining eyes. "What a sicko. First she accused Jason of raping her, even said Carson and I helped—"

"Jason Morris raped her?" Darius cut in.

"No!" Splotches of red broke out over Erin's face.

"That's what she *said*," Jackie inserted. "Total liar."

"I believe her account couldn't be substantiated," Detective Flannery smoothly explained. She glanced at Tresa. "I'm going to go to the station and question Megan Johnson. Ms. Morgan, care to join me?"

Tresa nodded and then hesitated, looking at Darius. "I'll see you back at the hotel?"

He didn't like it, but he knew she'd be safe in a police station, surrounded by cops. "Okay."

She followed Flannery to the car, looking over her shoulder at him once before ducking inside.

He knew he didn't have to worry, but he still did.

The pressure of Erin's hand on his arm increased and he looked down at her. "You'll give us a ride home after this, right?" She motioned to Jackie. "Carson picked us up tonight."

At the mention of her cousin, she started sobbing again. She burrowed her face against him, her arms wrapping around his waist. He patted her awkwardly on the back.

"Yeah. Sure," he replied, watching as Detective Flannery's taillights faded into the night. His chest tightened as Tresa moved farther and farther away from him.

He lifted his face, sniffing the air.

His gut squeezed and clenched. Nothing felt right. His skin tightened. Every sense kicked into hyper-alert. He glanced up at the waxing moon through the labyrinth of tree branches. Never had he felt its pull, its call. The thought of Tresa at risk, vulnerable, a slave to that fucking demon . . .

A savage heat burned through him. He was beyond agitated. His body couldn't shift without the full moon, but it wanted to. Just knowing Balthazar was out there . . .

He imagined he smelled him. The same scent he'd detected when he cornered him before—when he was in possession of Tresa. It was the familiar sickly sweet, loamy odor.

Detective Flannery's car vanished from view. He didn't like losing sight of Tresa. Not as long as Balthazar was out there, watching them, toying with them.

Somewhere in the back of his mind, he wondered when this had become about keeping Tresa safe. When had it ceased to be about himself and his freedom?

When had everything become about her?

NINETEEN

Tresa sipped the bitter coffee and winced. At least it was hot. The detectives had been interrogating Megan Johnson for hours now. Tresa had been observing through the one-way mirror, doing her best to get a read on the girl.

Darius had been right; she was one angry girl. Megan's expression revealed nothing. Her eyes stared blankly ahead as if nothing and no one was there. Her lips pressed in a flat, cold line.

There was a lot of pain inside her. And hate. It radiated off her. Tresa knew firsthand what pain and hate could lead a witch to do. The line she could cross if no one was around to keep her grounded. If no one was around to love her.

Flannery entered the observation room. She sighed and dropped a file folder on the table. "That's one messed-up girl in there. She's got plenty of motive. True or not, in her mind, Jason Morris raped her. The other vics all knew or helped in some way, according to her." Flannery released another sigh. "But we haven't got enough for an arrest. No physical evidence to link her. No witnesses."

Tresa shook her head in frustration and stared back at Megan through the glass. Her eyes were normal. She wasn't demon possessed right now, but that didn't mean she wasn't Balthazar's witch. "You're letting her go then?"

Tresa watched through the glass as Simpson entered the room with Megan and announced that she was free to go.

"We'll keep a close eye on her. She's not off the hook." Flannery looked pensive and uncertain as she watched Megan rise from her chair. The girl hid her arms inside the bulky sleeves of her sweater.

Tresa nodded, cold resolve sweeping through her. Yeah. So would she. So would *they*—she had Darius. Suddenly she felt lighter inside. She wasn't in this alone anymore. Whether it was Megan or not, they were close. Together, they'd find Balthazar and his witch.

She deliberately shied from thoughts of what came after that. When there was no more *they*.

* * *

TRESA GAVE A SLIGHT wave of thanks to the officer behind the wheel, watching as the police car drove away from the hotel. Dawn tinged the sky in soft shades of purple, but she didn't feel tired. The longer she lived, the less necessary sleep was. An unfortunate circumstance. In the long, empty years, where she had only her thoughts and an occasional pet to keep her company, she had yearned for the escape of sleep.

The hotel lobby was deserted save for the desk clerk. He smiled and gave her a nod of recognition as she moved to the elevator bank.

She pushed the button for floor 7 and waited, tapping her foot against the tiled floor. A slight breeze rustled the hair framing her face, warm enough for her to gasp and whirl around.

Her heart beat like a drum in her chest as she scanned the lobby. "Balthazar?" she whispered.

She peered at every shadow hugging the corners, trying to gauge whether it was more than a simple shadow, if the air hadn't just heated up a notch.

"You okay?" the desk clerk called out to her.

She nodded, trying to stop herself from shaking. After all these years, Balthazar could still strike terror in her heart. She hated that. It made her feel so weak. But she knew it would never change.

It was a sobering thought. Made everything in her life, in her future, seem pointless. A reminder that friends, relationships . . . love—she couldn't have any of that.

"Fine. Thank you." The elevator pinged open behind her. Turning, she stepped inside and punched 7.

On the short ride up, she struggled to settle her nerves. Walking down the corridor, she took several bracing breaths. She didn't want Darius to ask her a bunch of questions because she looked like a basket case. She was stronger than this.

She flexed her fingers around her key card, hesitating. How was she supposed to act around him? The last time they had been alone they had been all over each other. She couldn't expect that to continue. She bit her lip. She hoped he wouldn't try to talk about last night. Or apologize for what was clearly a one-night stand. That would be the worst. Sure, it had been a mistake, but if he actually said that—

The door opened before she finished the thought.

Darius stood on the other side, his large frame filling every inch of the doorway. She offered an awkward smile, acutely aware that this was the first time they were alone in this room since they'd made love.

He moved aside for her to enter. She walked in and dropped her bag on the chair. Then she turned around to recap the night at the police station, but he didn't give her the chance.

He pulled her into his arms and kissed her, his hands on either side of her face, holding her firmly but gently—as though he feared she would slip away.

The kiss consumed her. It felt like the kiss of someone denied a lifetime of kisses. Not like they had just been together hours ago. Her arms snaked around his neck.

Apparently last night hadn't been a one-time occurrence for him. He backed her into the bed, his hands working feverishly at her clothes as their bodies fell down together on the mattress. His mouth devoured hers, breaking away only long enough to pull her top over her head.

Next came her bra, her boots, her leggings. He left her for a moment and she blinked, dazed and panting, her body aching, arching, yearning for him.

"Darius," she cried hoarsely.

He was back before she finished his name.

"I'm here," he growled. Every hot, smooth

inch of him covered her. His flesh glided against hers, rough in certain spots and smooth in others. The air between them was charged, electric. His hand burned a path over her skin.

She sighed, breathed his name. It was as if he read her mind, knew what she wanted, what she liked. She moaned when he touched her neck, pressed his hot lips just behind her ear where he flesh was the most sensitive.

"Oh God, I love that . . ."

"What about this?" His dark head dipped to her breast.

She cried out when his wet mouth closed over her aching nipple.

A deep growl rumbled from his chest and she felt the vibration against her. It reminded her of what he was . . . what he wasn't. Still, it couldn't make her stop wrapping her legs around his hips and angling her pelvis to meet him. She squeezed an arm between them and closed her fingers around his erection.

"Tre." He dragged his mouth up her throat again.

She slid her hand up and down the length of him, her thumb rolling over his velvety head.

The flesh rippled over his clenched jaw. "Stop. Unless you want to finish this before I'm even inside you."

"You feel so good," she purred, positioning his cock against her, rubbing his head against her opening, letting her moisture tease him.

With a snarl that thrilled her to the bone, he seized her wrists and pressed them back onto the bed. Thrusting his face close, he nipped at her lips. "Witch."

She smiled up at him and nipped him back. "Don't like it? What are you going to do about it?"

His expression was savage in his need, those silver eyes of his afire. His hips settled firmly between her thighs, nudging them wider urgently.

She cried out with pleasure, arching her throat as he entered her, hard and swift, in one smooth stroke. Her body accepted his fullness, greedily adjusting to the invasion, her muscles tightening and clenching around his hard length.

He held himself perfectly still for one moment, a predator before the final pounce.

Together they basked in the union of their bodies. And then it was no longer enough. She worked her hips, taking him deeper, doing everything in her power to get him to move.

He bore down, pressing her hands deeper into the bed. He dropped his head, growling into the crook of her neck as he pulled himself almost fully free of her before lodging himself deep inside her again.

She bit into his shoulder, licked at the clean saltiness of his skin, and that enflamed him, pushing him over the edge. He pumped in and out of her, fast and deep, hitting that spot that made her come apart, writhe and buck beneath him. His hands released her wrists and his palms flattened over hers, his fingers lacing with hers as he drove into her again and again.

There was nothing soft or gentle about it, but she didn't want that. She wanted this. Wanted to be taken, wanted to be desired so desperately that there was no thought of softness or tenderness.

His hands finally slid free, gripping her hips and bringing her off the bed, better angling her hips for him.

Her hands moved of their own volition, gripped the taut cheeks of his ass in both hands. She clenched her inner muscles, pulled him to her and urged him on, faster.

There was only need.

He slid one hand beneath her hip, bringing her closer. His other hand slid beneath her neck, weaving up through her hair. With a slight tug on the strands, he pulled her head back, arching her throat for his lips, his open mouth hot on her skin. His teeth lightly grazed the cords of her neck, stopping directly over her sensitive pulse to suck and lave with his tongue. Her flesh turned to gooseflesh and she shivered, a moan swelling up from her throat.

His mouth devoured hers as he plunged in and out, loving her in a way completely unlike last night. This was uninhibited, with all the desperation of two wild animals. He took what he needed, pounding into her ruthlessly, and she didn't care because she wanted it, too. Needed it. Needed him.

Her hips rose to meet him and she cried out as he drove into her harder, clutching her hips as if she were a lifeline, the only thing keeping him grounded to earth.

Her heart swelled even as she reminded herself that this was only lust. It could never be anything more. Anything lasting. The memory of this would be all she had to keep for the countless years ahead.

It would have to be enough. She'd make it so.

Darius rolled to his back and pulled her close against his side, not giving her time to consider leaving him. He'd be fine staying in this bed with her indefinitely, unrealistic as that plan might be. For now, he'd let himself fantasize.

She held herself stiffly at first. Then she relaxed, her breath escaping in a soft gust as everything inside her eased and she melted against him. He stroked a hand up and down the elegant line of her spine.

He couldn't help touching her, holding her close. Almost like he thought she would disappear. He trailed his fingers up and down her bare arm in an easy stroke, languid and gentle.

"What happened to you?" she whispered. "You know, besides me . . . my curse?"

His hand stilled, her words an uncomfortable reminder of what she was and why he had set out to find her. It's not that he ever forgot. But without talking about it, he'd been able to ignore the ugly facts.

Everything came to a screeching stop inside him as the memories of the past washed through like acid.

"I don't talk about it." He never had. Who would he share it with? It's not like he had a life teeming with people. Friends and family were what others had—not him. Helen was the only one who truly cared about him, but he had never wished to burden her with the details of his past. She was already unaccountably bound to him. He didn't want to give her any more reason to pity him. He wanted her to feel free to leave him at any time.

"You know about me," she reasoned. "All of my foul deeds. You can't be nearly as awful."

"You're not awful," he replied, his voice gruff, his hand stroking her sweet flesh again. He propped himself up on an elbow and looked down at her, admiring her breasts. Not large, but a perfect fit for his palms. The dusky nipples. His mouth dried, hungering for their taste.

She gasped hoarsely as he played with them. "Fooled you, then, haven't I?"

He stroked a fingertip over one dusky nipple, enjoying the way it immediately pebbled. "You made a mistake."

"That's beyond generous of you." Her hand came to his chest. Her fingers played lightly against the flex of his muscles. "I made a *mistake* that's led to thousands dying and suffering. Seems like there should be another word for that." Before he could object, she continued, "It's your turn. What happened to you?"

He leaned down to suckle at one breast, his teeth nipping the turgid peak, stopping only when she was arching beneath him and thread-ing her fingers through his hair.

His gaze narrowed in on her face. "I was a monk."

She jerked slightly, lifting up on her elbows to look at him. "You were a religious man?"

"Does that surprise you?"

She stared at him with those brilliant eyes for a long moment, glancing down at her body, flushed from his lovemaking. "Umm . . ." Her voice faded.

He chuckled. Reaching down, he pushed her hair back behind her ear. "I was destined for Lindisfarne before I could even walk. My uncle was a monk there, and he visited me often when I was a boy. I was the youngest of my family. There were four brothers ahead of me. When I was eight years, my uncle took me. It was never asked of me what fate I pre-ferred. My parents were glad to see me gone and settled into a good and noble vocation." His mouth twisted. "One less mouth to feed."

"Did you like it there?"

"It was all I knew. The monastery and the farm." He shrugged one shoulder. It felt odd. This . . . sharing, *confiding*. "I was never a scholar. Not like the other brothers. I mostly worked the fields, brought in the crops that supported the monastery. We took in travelers . . . pilgrims. It was part of our service to God. Guests excited me. They'd been places. Seen things. Done things outside our little island." His chest tightened at the memory. "Almost laughable, isn't it? Considering I'll have seen . . . all I've done since?"

She stared at him thoughtfully for a long moment, her hair a fan of dark ink around her face. "We were all innocent once," she murmured. "Naïve in our own worlds."

He nodded. "Yeah." Looking into her eyes, he believed there was still a part of her that was innocent. He tasted it in her kiss. Something in her that was still good and pure. He couldn't feel this way about her otherwise.

Shaking his head, he pulled her to him and kissed her until he couldn't think anymore. Not about the past. Not about the future.

He slid his hands down the smooth slope of her back, his fingers gliding over each bump of her vertebrae, delighting in the sensation of her silky skin against his palms.

Tresa, like this, hot and wanting in his arms, was the only thing he cared about right now.

TWENTY

It was midday before they forced themselves from the hotel room. They'd ordered room service and eaten in bed, wearing nothing but the hotel's plush robes. Sharing an enormous plate of Belgian waffles dripping with maple syrup, Tresa had fooled herself into believing that the outside world had ceased to exist. That they could stay lovers forever.

A fantasy that was dashed the moment she stepped over the threshold. It felt like she was leaving behind the last bit of pleasure and happiness she'd ever have again.

With one last glance over her shoulder at the rumpled bed, she turned back around. She didn't want to leave the sanctuary of this room—didn't want to make it just a memory and put it in the past with every other good thing that had ever happened to her.

She wanted to freeze herself in this moment with Darius forever. She hadn't thought she'd have this. She didn't deserve it, but now that she had experienced this happiness . . . she didn't know how she was going to survive the next thousand years without it.

Darius took her hand as they moved down the hall and stepped inside the elevator. It was easy and automatic, like they were any other couple. Already she knew his touch so well, the texture of his skin, the shape of his hand against her own.

She glanced at him a few times, trying to reconcile him with the furious lycan who'd crashed into her world. He walked beside her, holding her hand as if this was the most normal thing in the world. His expression was relaxed, peaceful, the hard lines less severe— nothing like the man who'd been so eager to destroy her.

"You ready for this?" he asked when they were in the car, heading into a part of the city she hadn't yet seen. The GPS announced the directions.

She nodded. They had agreed on what needed to be done. Her stomach clenched at the thought, because it meant moving forward, reaching a resolution and putting this intimacy between them to a halt. Tresa was wise enough to know that when the witch was captured, she herself would return to avoiding Balthazar in subarctic climates. And Darius . . . Well, he had his own demons to avoid—namely himself, each and every full moon.

It started to drizzle. She watched the windshield wipers move from side to side rhythmically. "Do you think it's Megan Johnson?"

"I only saw her for those few moments, but she definitely didn't look like the rest of the people at that party."

"Yeah, she wasn't there to mourn Jason Morris," Tresa agreed. "And she wasn't broken up over Carson, either."

"Whoever the witch is, she's going to kill again soon. Either because she wants to or because Balthazar wants her to."

"If Megan Johnson *isn't* the witch, then it's somehow connected to her. Whether she even realizes it. All the victims are connected to her. Maybe an angry friend? Sister? Her mother, even?"

Darius nodded thoughtfully. The headlights of an oncoming car flashed across his face. The sky had darkened with the rain and most vehicles had turned on their lights. "Whatever the case, she's the only suspect we have and we can't leave her to her own devices."

The GPS indicated that they needed to take

the next exit. He scanned the low-income housing and warehouses they passed. "Not the nicest neighborhood."

Tresa looked out the window as they passed a homeless woman pushing a shopping cart. Her drenched hat hung low over her face, beyond the point of protecting her from the deluge. "No dorms out here."

"Maybe she prefers this to living on campus. From what you told me she said during the interrogation, she feels betrayed. Not just by Jason, Carson and Erin, but the entire university."

"Yeah. She had no problem expressing how pissed she was at Erin and the victims."

Tresa understood how rage and betrayal could drive people to do something they normally wouldn't. Tresa believed Megan Johnson had been raped. The pain she'd read in Megan's eyes through the one-way glass . . . that couldn't be faked. Tresa felt sorry for her . . . until the images from her nightmares flooded her, and then she recalled the horrible way those people had suffered, too.

They pulled up in front of a run-down apartment complex. Several people loitered on the street. A man staggered down the broken sidewalk, drinking from a brown paper bag.

A cluster of older boys hung out on the corner, shooting them calculating looks as they parked.

Darius killed the engine and sat eerily still behind the wheel.

Tresa glanced at his profile, noting the tension locking his jaw. She tested his name uncertainly.

He turned abruptly to face her in the seat. "We can leave."

She blinked. "What do you mean?"

He motioned toward the building. "I don't want you anywhere close to Balthazar. I don't even want you in the same city anymore."

She knew he was recalling coming face-to-face with her under Balthazar's possession. She hated that he had seen her like that.

She released a small sigh and sank back in the seat with a squeak of leather. "Darius . . . he owns me. It is what it is."

"No," he ground out, grabbing her hand, holding tight. "Don't say that. He doesn't own you."

She held his gaze, her voice sharp. "Yes. He does. I don't like it, but it's true. It's been that way for over two thousand years. Just because he's not in possession of me right this minute doesn't mean I'm free."

"He's got her." He waved at the building.

She shook her head. "So what are you saying? We should just forget about her . . . and everyone she's killing? I can't do that. And I don't believe you want to do that, either."

"Don't mistake me for noble," he spat. Disengaging his hand, he dragged it through his dark hair. "You more than anyone else should know what I am. You made me into this."

She jerked as though slapped, a small hiss of air shuddering from her. After last night she had thought that they were past that, but they never would be. It would never leave. She was not to be forgiven . . . her actions never forgotten.

Inhaling a deep, shuddery breath, she regained her composure and moistened her lips. "What are we doing here, Darius? It's clear that when it comes to me, you can never forgive and forget . . ."

His eyes fastened hotly on her, searing her in her seat. He reached across the space separating them, slipped his hand around her nape and hauled her closer for a blistering kiss. His lips, his tongue, his teeth took hers, claimed her, left her shaking, moaning, clutching his shoulders.

When they finally broke for air, he muttered against her mouth, "I couldn't do that to you if I didn't forgive you for the past."

Their heavy breaths mingled. His forehead rested against hers. Her hands had yet to ease their grip on his shoulders. After a long moment, he slid his hand from around her neck and stared out the window again at Megan Johnson's apartment.

It took everything inside her not to pull him back for more. He made her crazy. Made her forget her purpose. Made her want to crawl on top of him and never come up for air again.

He drew in a deep breath. "As long as he has her to bend to his will, he'll leave you alone."

She closed her eyes in a long blink, wishing she could do what he was suggesting. Turn and walk away. If only it were that simple. "And could I just live my life? Endure the nightmares and pretend I don't know the things she's doing? I can't do that."

"Damnit, Tre." He slapped the steering wheel. "You can't have lived this long without watching people die all the time. In the blink of an eye. It strikes where it will. Mortal life is fleeting. You can't stop that."

And yet they both craved mortal life so badly. Wished to be who they once were before they'd turned into monsters. Despite his words, she knew he treasured life just as much as she did.

"But I can," she insisted, not accepting his

justification. "This time, I can stop it. Or at least delay its happening prematurely."

"At the cost of yourself!" He shook his head fiercely and turned in his seat, his hands cradling her face. "Do you know how long I've been alone?"

She stared at him, stunned, her heart aching at the emotion in his voice . . . his face.

She replied in a voice that trembled terribly, "Not as long as I have."

He searched her face for a long moment, but some of the heat left him as he whispered, "And you'll settle for that?"

"I haven't any choice. I can't pretend that I deserve some fairy-tale existence. That's not for me." She held her breath, almost adding, *and it's not for you*. But he knew that. Deep down in his core. She didn't need to pour salt in the wound and remind him that he was every bit as cursed as she was.

The light in his eyes dulled as his hands slipped from her face. He nodded in defeat and she almost wanted to weep, to beg him not to give up on the idea, the *dream* of them, even though that's what she had demanded. She didn't want the fantasy to die.

"That's the way it is then." He faced the front again, grimly staring out the windshield

at Megan Johnson's apartment just as a gun-
shot shattered the quiet.

THE SOUND OF THE shot echoed in the late
afternoon, reverberating off the buildings.
Darius tensed, looking for a shooter or a
victim, but Tresa was out of the car and
running across the street before he'd decided
on his next move.

"Shit." Flinging open the door, he took off
after her, catching up with her in an instant. He
pulled her to a stop just before the building's
front door.

"What are you doing?" he growled, furious that she was running headlong into danger
with no thought of herself.

Her gaze was wild. "She's in there—she
could be hurting someone! I can't let her do
that again!"

"Just think for a second. Since when is a gun
her weapon of choice?" He gave her a gentle
shake.

Comprehension flickered over her panicked
face. She exhaled heavily and nodded, her dark
hair swaying around her shoulders. "Yeah.
Okay. Okay."

"You've got to slow down and think. Stop

putting yourself in harm's way." His hands trembled a little on her shoulders. He quickly dropped them to his sides, hating that he should feel so weak and unmanned. It had been so long since he'd actually felt this way for another person. Since he'd *cared* this much. It was what he'd wanted, what he had missed for so long. Now he had it, and he couldn't help thinking how much easier everything had been before. When there was nothing and no one to worry over. Fear for her was an unsettling thing, a beast gnawing at his heart.

Shaking his head, he refocused his attention on Tresa.

"Okay," she breathed. "I'll be careful." She motioned to the graffiti-sprayed door. "Let's go."

Taking Tresa's hand, he pulled her behind him and stepped inside, his eyes adjusting to the dark interior and peering around them. Only a silver bullet could do permanent damage to him, but that didn't mean an average bullet wouldn't debilitate him. If he was incapacitated, then he was just dead weight for Tresa.

He moved cautiously. The dim hallway was full of shadows. Somewhere, a baby cried; otherwise it was eerily quiet. Still. Like gunfire was nothing new, and the tenants knew they needed to stay inside until the smoke cleared.

"Apartment three sixteen," she whispered at his back. Nodding, he led them up the stairway, not about to take the questionable elevator.

The sound of the crying baby grew louder on the third floor. They passed a door and could hear a mother making shushing sounds inside.

They stopped in front of Megan Johnson's apartment. The door was cracked open. Darius started to push it open with the flat of his hand, holding his breath as it began to swing inward, hoping he wasn't about to feel a bullet rip through him.

He felt Tresa behind him, straining for a glimpse inside. "Can you see—"

Something whizzed past his head and a vase exploded against the wall, shards of ceramic shooting everywhere. He saw a slight figure sliding out the window at the far end of the corridor and was lurching in that direction until he felt Tresa tugging on his arm, pulling him back.

"Darius, look!"

He followed Tresa's gaze.

Erin painstakingly picked herself up from the floor of the apartment, one hand covering her nose. Blood seeped out from her fingers and ran over her lip.

Tresa rushed inside the room to help her, looping an arm around her waist. "Are you okay?" She bent her head to better see her face. "What happened? What are you doing here?"

Darius dove back into the hall. Running down the corridor, his feet barely touching the floor, he jerked to a stop to peer out the window. He watched a black-clad figure deftly climb down the fire escape. Once at ground level, she looked up at him, confirming his suspicions. It was Megan Johnson.

He watched her race off and was on the verge of following her when he heard Tresa cry out sharply.

Forgetting about Megan, he sprinted back to the apartment, fear lodged in his throat.

Tresa was sprawled on the grimy floor. She looked up at him, holding her cheek.

"What happened?" Darius crouched before her, peeling her hand from her face. Her pale cheek was marred an angry red.

She waved a hand at Erin. "She clocked me. Just surprised me; I'll be fine."

"You stopped me from going after that bitch!" Erin said defensively, delicately pinching her bleeding nose. "Where did Megan go?"

Darius glared at her. "She got away. Took off down the fire escape."

"Great!" Erin threw her arms up in the air.

"Probably because you decided to take a shot at her." Tresa dangled in the air a handgun that presumably belonged to Erin.

Darius snatched the gun and turned incredulous eyes on the girl. "Are you serious?"

Erin's eyes sparked with defiance. "I wanted her to admit what she did."

Darius swore as he stuffed the gun into his pocket. "You're lucky she only punched you. You have no idea what she's capable of."

"She's killing my friends—I think I do know!" Indignant color burned brightly across Erin's cheeks as she clutched her nose.

Tresa patted her arm. "Calm down."

Darius shook his head in disgust. "Let's get out of here before the cops show up." They needed to catch up with Megan. No telling what she would do now that she knew they were on to her.

He led Tresa and Erin out of the building. "Where's your car?"

Erin motioned to a BMW parked across the street. "But I don't think I can drive." She lifted her hand from her nose and flashed her bloodied fingers, as if that prevented her from driving.

Darius sighed. He looked at Tresa, but she

was already holding out her hand for the keys to the rental. "It's okay. You drive her. I'll follow."

He dropped the keys into her palm. She turned and unlocked the car without a word. He watched her until Erin tugged on his arm, pulling him toward her car.

"I'm so glad you're here." Her clutch on his arm was becoming a familiar sensation.

Settling behind the wheel, he glanced in the rearview mirror. The need to see Tresa, to keep her in his sights at all times, to always keep her close to him, was becoming more and more powerful.

TWENTY-ONE

Erin lived in a lavish condominium with two other girls. As they walked down the plum carpet–lined corridor, Tresa couldn't help but compare it to Megan Johnson's squalid environment. Erin punched in her door code and entered the airy apartment.

"My roommates are in class right now," she announced, dropping her purse on the couch.

His expression grim, Darius asked, "What were you thinking, going to Megan Johnson's place today? Armed with a gun?"

Erin look affronted. Her lips pulled into a childlike pout as she crossed her arms over her chest. "I wasn't going to kill her. Have some faith. I just wanted to spook her into admitting what she did."

Tresa rolled her eyes. "And then what? So she admits it to you—what would you do next?"

Erin's faced flushed. She glared at Tresa and

then stormed into the kitchen. She returned a moment later, a bottle of sparkling water in her hand. Arching an eyebrow, she took a dainty sip.

"You've got to stay out of this," Darius continued, his voice hard.

Tresa pointed to Erin's nose. The bleeding had stopped, but it was pink and swollen. Faint traces of dried blood ran in streaks above her lip. "She already hurt you."

The pink in Erin's cheeks deepened. "She knocked the gun from my hands and hit me," she mumbled.

"Look," Darius said in a gentler voice, moving forward and resting a hand on her shoulder. "We don't want you hurt. Enough people have already died. Let us take care of this."

Her expression softened and Tresa suspected it had a bit to do with his hand on her shoulder. She knew the power behind Darius's touch. The girl was obviously infatuated with him. He either didn't see it or pretended not to.

Erin inhaled, lifting her prominent chest higher. "All right." She gave him a wobbly smile. "I know you care about me, and I don't want you distracted by worrying over me. Not while you're tracking down Megan."

Tresa swallowed a snort.

"Thank you." Darius guided Tresa toward the door.

Tresa opened the door and stepped into the hall. When she realized Darius wasn't with her, she turned around just in time to see Erin wrap her body around him like a second skin. She mashed her mouth to his as if she was starved for the taste of him.

He didn't seem to be fighting her, and Tresa stalked down the hallway, hating that she could feel so *jealous*.

"Tre!"

She ignored Darius, keeping a steady pace. No running. That would look as though she was hurt and upset. And she wasn't so foolish as to give him that much power over her. No way.

A hand clamped on her arm and forced her around. "Didn't you hear me calling you?"

"Of course. I have perfectly good hearing," she said stiffly. "I have excellent vision, too."

His gaze scanned her face, missing nothing. He motioned behind him. "You're not upset about that?"

She tried for a light laugh. "What? You swapping spit with some college girl? Why would that upset me? You can do whatever you want with whomever you want."

He dropped his hand from her arm. "You

think I *wanted* her to kiss me? I just asked you to run away with me!"

And she had said no. A fact she needed to remember.

She crossed her arms and shrugged. "I have no claim on you."

He pulled back, his expression intense, probing. "So you don't care. I could go in there and fuck that girl, and you wouldn't care."

She winced, but forced a stiff nod.

"Well, I *want* you to care."

"Don't say that," she hissed.

"Too late." He pounced, his mouth claiming hers. He kissed her long and hard. Her hands came up to cling to his wrists—at first to pull them away, but that thought quickly fled.

She melted into him, relishing his hardness, his strength. She marveled at how she could feel both safe and excited, like she was hanging from the edge of a cliff.

When he tore his lips from hers, she strained forward, chasing his lips, seeking the drugging taste and warmth of him. She felt dazed, lost, staring into the gleam of his eyes.

He smiled down at her, tucking her hair behind her ear. "How can you doubt that I care more about you than about some vapid girl with more lip gloss than brains?"

At the sound of a soft gasp, Tresa looked past Darius and saw Erin at the end of the hallway, her expression shattered.

Darius turned as Erin whirled around and raced back into her apartment. The door slammed.

Tresa winced. "Should we—"

"Let her go. We have bigger concerns—the first being Megan Johnson."

"And if she's our witch, I think Erin just moved to the top of her list. We'd better stake out Erin's condo. I doubt she'll let us camp out in her living room now."

Darius nodded. "Yeah."

Tresa headed for the car, tossing up the keys and catching them in her hand. "We're going to need some coffee."

Twenty-two

Tresa wadded up the trash on the floorboard and stuffed it into a wrinkled plastic bag. Finished, she took a sip of her tepid coffee to wash down her last Cheeto. Over the last few hours, she'd eaten her way through Ding Dongs and various types of chips.

Darius shook his head. "How can you eat that stuff?"

"Don't tell me you miss the food we used to eat?" She made a face as she set her coffee cup in the holder. "I don't know what I did before preservatives." Her eyes widened. "Before chocolate. Besides, this is a stakeout. Aren't we supposed to snack on junk food?"

He couldn't help but smile. "Snack, yes. Binge?"

She winked. "Just don't let me anywhere near a waffle house. Now, *that* might be the most marvelous invention of modern man."

He nodded, feigning seriousness. "Yeah.

Forget about the pacemaker, vaccinations and space travel . . ."

Her expression turned equally serious. "Nothing tops the waffle house." She held up a hand. "Wait. Except maybe the Slinky."

He nodded firmly. "Ah. The Slinky. Of course."

She finally grinned.

Everything inside him lifted, lightening at the glow of that smile. All of him felt touched by it, warmed and comforted. He couldn't remember ever feeling this way. Not even when he was at the monastery and he had people around him who cared. In their own way. As much as his fellow monks could care. That life had been grueling, hard and joyless. This, with Tresa, was the closest he had come to joy.

His cell phone rang, and he glanced down to see who was calling: Helen.

Tresa did her best to look uninterested, but he saw her sneak a glimpse at the caller name.

He answered the phone. "Yes."

"Darius! Heavens, where are you? Have you looked at the calendar? The moon is waxing."

Tresa tried to appear interested in the non-existent activity across the street, but her eyes shifted to him several times.

"I know," Darius told Helen patiently. He was *always* attuned to the status of the moon.

Helen continued with her concerns, chastising him about not getting home at once, her voice a buzzing gnat in his ear.

Tresa carefully ate a chip, biting off the corners one at a time.

At last Darius erupted. "I'm perfectly aware of how much time I have left. It's not something I can forget. Don't worry. I'll be home in time. I'll call you when I'm headed back." He ended the call before Helen could object further.

"Home?" Tresa looked at him, her dark eyebrow lifted in question.

The word from her lips jarred him. Yes. He had a home of sorts. Or at least a home base.

"Believe it or not, yeah. I haven't spent my entire life chasing you." He attempted a teasing tone, but missed the mark.

Color stained her cheeks and she laughed brokenly. "Of course not. Just because I never lived anywhere very long doesn't mean you didn't put down roots. It doesn't mean you don't have someone waiting for you back home . . ." Her gaze drifted out to the street again, as if she couldn't meet his gaze. "Wherever that is." She stuffed another chip in her mouth.

"That was Helen," he explained. "She's . . . my housekeeper, I guess. Seems a bit inadequate to call her that, I suppose."

She shot him a dubious look. "I see. A housekeeper who calls to check up on you."

"She's a worrier. Always has been. She's been with me for close to forty years now."

Tresa settled her gaze back on him again. "That long? She's human?"

"Yes. She's the grandmother I never had."

Instantly, her voice softened. "It must be nice . . . having someone care about where you are. Having someone care, period."

"I saved her when she was a young woman. A few lycans thought they'd make her their toy for the night. She's been with me ever since. It's nice to be around someone who knows what I am and accepts me anyway."

"Yeah," Tresa murmured, looking at him in a way that made him uncomfortable—as if he was some kind of hero. If only she knew all the terrible things he had done . . . things so terrible, nothing he ever did now could make up for them.

"It *is* nice having someone accept you for who you are," she added.

Meaning she thought he accepted her, even when he shouldn't. And he did. He had for some time. Their gazes held for a long moment. Tension crackled between them.

He looked down to the bag of chips crumpled in her lap. "You know, you're addicted to junk food," he remarked, needing a break in the spell.

"True." She shrugged, unbothered. "It's not as though it's going to kill me. And I definitely don't miss cleaning the game Michel used to bring home each day."

Her husband. A silence fell between them as he wondered about the man she had clearly loved.

She slid him a look before staring back out at Erin's condo. "Was there ever anyone for you? Before? Or after . . ."

Before the curse that ruined your life. The curse I created. She didn't need to say it; he heard it nonetheless.

"Not too many women at the monastery. And the brothers never permitted females within the walls." His lips twisted. "After the pack . . . after that there were women."

Her smile slipped and he was certain she knew that he was remembering the brutality of those years.

"Do you ever think He remembers us?" she whispered.

Maybe she thought Darius would have an answer because he had been at the monastery, a servant of God. "I don't know. I guess that's why I keep trying to break the curse. I can't ever be the man I once was, but maybe there's a way to reclaim something of myself. Even just a shred."

"Do you think . . . there's any chance of redemption for us?"

He stroked her cheek with one finger. "You deserve it, Tre." He knew she had never hoped for it before—never thought that she deserved it.

She gave a small nod. "I feel different now. Changed." Her gaze locked with his. "You've done that. Made me hope."

He sighed. "I was lost for so long. I did so many evil things . . . I don't know if I can be forgiven. But if I regain my mortality, I'll face whatever is waiting for me. Even if that's damnation."

"No." She covered his hand with hers, pressing it against her cheek. "Just thinking that you . . ." She shuddered. "I can handle the thought of my damnation, but not yours."

He inhaled a sharp breath.

Suddenly her eyes widened, as if realizing the implications of what she'd said.

Darius smiled slowly, satisfied in a way he

hadn't felt in . . . well, ever. "It sounds as if you care about me, Tresa." He cocked an eyebrow. "Maybe even more than care."

HIS WORDS ECHOED THROUGH her mind, weaving dangerously around her heart, shaking her to the core.

She stared at him with wide eyes, astonished that she had revealed so much. Astonished that she was in this situation at all—feeling these things for a lycan. She moved her lips, but could summon no words.

It had been so long since she'd valued someone over herself. Since she had felt love. The realization hit her like a slap. *She loved him.*

And he knew it.

"Look," Darius said.

She snapped to attention as he pointed to a shadow skulking by the hedges along the side of the stucco building.

"Is it her?" She straightened in her seat.

"Too dark to tell," he muttered.

She moved to open her door. His hand on her arm stopped her. "Wait here."

She tensed, scowling. "What? No way. I'm—"

"If it's her, Balthazar might be in control at the moment."

"Yeah." She nodded in agreement. "And you could use my help."

"I don't need to worry about you, too. I don't want you near him." His stare drilled into her.

She swallowed, shaken by the intensity of his gaze. "So I'm just going to sit this out from now on? Let you take all the risks?"

He opened his mouth and then shut it, clearly unsure as to what answer worked here.

She watched the shadowed figure move behind the condo, fading from sight. Anxiety tripped through her. "Fine. Go. Before we lose sight of her."

Slumping back in her seat, she watched as Darius jogged across the street. For a moment she debated following him, but creeping up behind him might be the kind of distraction that put him in danger. Seconds ticked by as her nerves stretched taut, her stomach dipping and twisting until she felt sick.

A realization took over. Balthazar knew what Darius was. He could make sure his witch did, too, and arm her with a silver bullet.

And she was sitting in this stupid car because he wanted her out of harm's way. *Hell, no.*

With a hoarse sound, she fumbled for the door handle and stumbled out of the car. She'd just move in close enough to see if she could *feel* Balthazar's presence.

She dashed across the street, her heart pounding a desperate rhythm in her chest. Her only thought as she rounded the house was to reach Darius, to make sure nothing happened to him. It didn't occur to her to wonder what she would do if she did sense Balthazar. Because at that point he would sense her, too. She'd be doing exactly what Darius didn't want—putting herself within the demon's range.

She heard footsteps behind her and she whirled around, getting only a glimpse of a dark figure before something swung at her head and her world exploded in pain.

Bright spots danced before her eyes as she fell, holding an arm over her face instinctively to ward off another blow. But this time she was kicked in the ribs. A sharp breath whooshed from her lungs and she curled into a tight ball.

She concentrated on the foot swinging her way, willing all her energy into stopping it from making contact. She propelled the oncoming leg so far up, her attacker fell backward with a sharp cry. A sharp *feminine* cry. Balthazar's witch?

They moved simultaneously, getting quickly to their feet. Tresa crouched low, every muscle tense and ready to spring. She sniffed the air, lifting her face, trying to detect Balthazar. Nothing. He wasn't here.

So it was just the two of them. Two demon witches.

"I've been eager to meet you." She spoke into the dark, addressing the faceless female who'd occupied her nightmares for weeks now.

The witch didn't respond. Her shadowy figure continued to circle Tresa, moving with cat-like grace.

Tresa tried again. "This isn't you. It's him. Balthazar. You didn't want to hurt those people."

A soft chuckle floated on the air. Eerie and faint.

There was a click, almost imperceptible, and suddenly a sharp burning sensation stabbed Tresa in the chest. Her hand flew there, grasping the slim object protruding from her breast. With a grunt, she pulled it free.

She peered at it in the dark, unable to see it clearly. It felt like some kind of . . . dart. A tranq? She felt it carefully with all her fingers, discovering wet blood at the pointy tip.

And then everything blurred.

The dark swirled around her and she dropped to one knee with a bruising jar. She fell onto her other knee next. The object slipped from her fingers as the ground rose up to smack her in the face. Then she was nose deep in loamy earth.

Steps crunched near her face. Her breath wheezed strangely from her lips, stirring the moist soil.

A hand touched the back of her head, stroking, petting her almost tenderly. An incredible sense of lethargy stole over her.

As everything slowed and dulled, the world slipping away, she heard a voice say, "What makes you think I don't enjoy hurting people?"

Darius watched the female crouching at Erin's back window. She moved on to another window, a satchel bumping her hip as she tried to peer between the blinds. She wasn't very stealthy, trampling over the flower beds, muttering beneath her breath at the mud on her shoes. He was almost surprised she'd gotten the upper hand over Erin. Then again, she had Balthazar at her disposal.

A dark rope of hair snaked out of the hood of her sweatshirt, and as she angled toward the light he saw her profile. It was Megan.

When she started to fumble inside her bag, he moved forward and seized her by the back of the neck, stopping her before she could pull out a weapon.

She squeaked and spun around, her hands lashing out, as harmless as a flurry of moths.

"Let me go," she panted, her eyes as wild as any hunted animal's. Clearly, she wasn't under Balthazar's influence at the moment.

He hung on to her with one hand, his other hand delving inside her bag. She pelted him with her free hand, her punches bouncing off him.

Some of the fight left her when he pulled out a can of spray paint. "What's this?" he demanded.

"What's it look like?" she snarled. "I'm gonna teach Erin and her bitch roommates a lesson. They laughed at me . . . looked the other way. Erin knew—" She choked on a sob, her hand flying to her mouth to cover the sound. Tears streamed down her face. He saw, *felt*, her raw pain.

"She knew what Jason was doing to me in that room, and she didn't care. She didn't try to stop him."

"So what were you going to do with this?" He stared at the can of spray paint. Hardly the weapon of a killer bent on vengeance.

"What do you think I was going to do?" She looked at him as if he was an idiot. "I was going to spray-paint the house."

Staring at her, he accepted the fact that he wasn't looking at the face of a killer. Not even close.

The obvious conclusion came next. If she wasn't the killer, then the killer was still out there.

"Tresa." Her name escaped him without thought. Foreboding crawled up and over his scalp, and he released Megan. Turning, he raced back to the street in a flash of wind.

The car still sat there, but Tresa wasn't in it. He backtracked, every sense alive, straining for any sight or scent of her as he studied his surroundings.

Suddenly he stopped. The coppery aroma of blood filled his nose. He got down on the ground and patted the grass until his fingertips met something besides mud and rainwater.

Leaning back on his heels, he rubbed his fingers together, testing the slick moisture, knowing what it was even before he brought it to his nose for a sniff.

Blood.

Tresa's blood.

He dropped his head into his hands, pulling at the strands until they felt close to ripping from the roots.

She was gone. He'd lost her.

Twenty-three

Tresa came awake slowly, sensation returning to her limbs gradually, chasing away the needles-and-pins feeling. Coherent thoughts formed slowly, drifting like wispy clouds. Her breastbone ached where the tranquilizer had hit her, but she resisted the urge to rub it. She didn't want to alert her captor yet to the fact that she was awake.

She listened, trying to gauge whether or not she was alone. After several moments of suffocating silence, she cracked open one eye. Gray brick walls stared back at her. She was lying on a mattress. In an empty room. She rotated her neck, seeing one window covered with cheap blinds. No light spilled inside.

Confident she was alone, she tried to raise up only to fall back down. The ropes at her wrists and ankles stopped her from moving more than a half inch.

She held herself still, staring at the cracked

plaster above her. Darius wouldn't know what had happened to her. And her stomach lurched sickly as she realized that this was just like the settings in her dreams . . . and that now she was the victim. Her gaze slid left and right, searching for any possible way to save herself.

Nothing but a built-in particleboard dresser. A closet with a sliding door hanging off the track. It looked like an empty dorm room. She lifted her head to peer out the blinds. A vacant parking lot. She dropped her head back down on the mattress and strained for any sounds coming from inside the building. Voices. A door slamming. Footsteps.

Nothing. Thick silence.

Turning her head, she closed her eyes in anguish. The witch had stashed her here in total isolation. Wherever she'd gone, she'd be back. And Tresa didn't doubt her fate. She knew what Balthazar wanted. It was what he'd always wanted. *Freedom*.

Once she was dead, he'd have the ability to take corporeal form and walk this earth. He could do what he wanted, when he wanted, without having to manipulate an unwilling witch—like her.

Lying here, defenseless, she was a lamb for the slaughter. It would be a simple matter for

Balthazar to get his way. His new witch just had to decapitate her.

In the distance, a door slammed shut. It sounded like it came from below somewhere—a bottom floor. She held her breath as she listened. Every part of her trembled, her heart beating like a fierce drum inside her chest. The footsteps started out faintly, growing louder until they were a steady tread drawing closer and closer.

She rested her cheek on the mattress, watching the handle turn and the door swing open with a creak of protest. Tresa didn't know what frightened her more. The prospect of finally coming face-to-face with the witch whose mind she had stepped inside during all her horrible murders? She knew the evil that lurked in her. The absolute lack of emotion. *Or* confronting Balthazar again? Even if he didn't currently possess his witch, he'd be along soon enough.

Her gaze settled on the woman's face and shock rippled through her. She should have known. Should have sensed something in her.

"Flannery," she breathed. Maybe the detective had been too quick to believe her. Maybe she'd brought her into the investigation too readily. Tresa should have known. Should have recognized her for what she was.

"You finally woke up." She closed the door behind her. "I got tired of waiting and decided to go get a latte and a bite to eat."

Tresa gazed at her, seeing the real Flannery for the first time. Her eyes were their usual shade of brown, not the soulless black that meant Balthazar was in residence. Tresa scanned the room, looking for his shadow.

"He's not here," Flannery replied affably as she sat on the edge of the mattress. As if this was a friendly visit. Dropping a brown paper bag beside her, she wrapped her fingers around her cardboard coffee cup and took a deep sip.

"Mmm," she moaned appreciatively. "That's good stuff. Better than the tar back at the station."

She turned her attention to the bag and pulled out an enormous chocolate chip muffin. "These are so good." Flannery tore off a corner and chewed it with a moan of appreciation. "Course, I'll have to make up for it at the gym later."

"Why?"

Flannery looked at her. "Never know when I'll be chasing down a perp."

"No. *Why* are you involved with Balthazar?"

"Ah, of course. *That* why." She waved her hand in a small circle. "Why did I bring you here?

Why did I kill all those people? Why did I give myself over to Balthazar?" She snorted. "I think the answer to that last one is obvious. I mean, you did the same thing, right? You tell me."

Tresa considered why she had surrendered her soul to Balthazar, the horror of that day . . .

"Well? Why'd you do it?" Flannery stared at Tresa as if she was really interested. "Was it the power? The immortality?" She motioned to her body. "I'll get to be young forever. Nothing wrong with that."

Tresa's cheeks heated with indignation. She had not given herself to Balthazar for reasons so shallow. "I didn't care about that." She was nothing like Flannery. Nothing. "My family was murdered. Balthazar offered me revenge. I was stupid, overcome with grief."

Flannery nodded, her expression far away. "Revenge. Yeah. That was a perk for me, too." She blinked as though snapping from her reflections. "I met Jason a year ago. He charmed me." A hint of a smile brushed her lips. "He got off on the idea of fucking a cop. He liked me to wear my holster when we did it." The softness in her gaze turned hard. "I covered for Jason, saved his ass from arrest. And then he kept getting with other girls when he promised it was just me."

"He raped Megan Johnson."

Flannery's eyes flashed. "She asked for it. She threw herself at him."

"Hannah? Shannan? The others? Why did you kill them?"

"I took care of Hannah to send him a message."

"Apparently it didn't work."

She glared at Tresa.

"What about Carson?"

"A loose end. He'd seen me with Jason."

"And Shannan?" she pressed. "Was she another message for Jason?"

"She was a stupid bitch. I saw her flirting with Jason. I pulled her over and warned her to back off, and she just laughed at me. I showed her."

"You took revenge."

She nodded. "Just like you."

"We're nothing alike."

Flannery's eyes turned to ice. "That's right. I'm better. That's why Balthazar chose me."

"Balthazar chose you because you're evil. Like him."

She shrugged, clearly unoffended. She shook off the crumbs from her fingers. "Yeah. Well. I'm not the one tied to a bed, about to have my head cut off."

Tresa jerked at this announcement.

Flannery smiled broadly, her white teeth a sharp contrast against her tanned skin. She made a cutting motion against her neck.

Tresa inhaled a ragged breath, fighting for control over her emotions. Fear, desperation, and clawing panic threatened to choke her.

Somewhere, in the back of her mind, she realized she would have reacted differently a year ago. Even a few months ago. Before Darius.

All these years, she had fought death to keep Balthazar from gaining corporeal form. That was the only reason she'd stayed alive. It was her responsibility to the world. She had no one. No one to love her. No one she loved back.

Even when the loneliness ate at her, and the misery of her memories gnawed at her, she'd resisted ending her own life. Because she had to.

But now things were different. She had someone she wanted to get back to.

Panic crawled hotly over her skin. She wanted to lash out, to shout, to scream. She sucked in a deep breath, fighting for calm. Now wasn't the time to lose it.

Grasping for something to keep Flannery talking, she asked, "What's your gift? Your power?" Every witch had one. It was what attracted a demon, like a huge blinking light over your head.

Flannery scowled, as if this was a sore point. "Not anything useful. That's why I need Balthazar. Without him, I might as well be nothing."

Tresa shook her head, moistening her lips. "I don't believe that—"

"I had the touch. I could heal people," she snapped, her expression annoyed. "Like I said. Useless."

Tresa stared at her, marveling at the bitter irony. She could heal with a touch, but instead she was killing people. "Why would you think that was useless?"

Flannery flattened a palm against her chest. "What does that get me? Nothing. Balthazar showed me the way. He gave me true power."

Balthazar or no, this woman had been destined for a dangerous path. But *with* Balthazar, she was a sociopath.

Her thoughts spinning, Tresa forced a smile. "So he actually convinced you to cut my head off, did he?" She managed a chuckle. "Wow. I didn't think you were that stupid."

Flannery slowly lowered her muffin to the bag on her lap, her eyes narrowing. "What does that mean?"

"Kill me and you lose him. He'll be free. He might even turn on you." She tried to shrug despite the ropes binding her. "He won't need you anymore. He'll have corporeal form, be free to wander the earth."

Flannery blinked slowly, processing this.

"Yep. You can kiss immortality good-bye. You'll just go back to being you. And all he promised you will be gone. Guess he didn't explain that, did he?"

Flannery knocked the muffin bag aside and jumped up to storm back and forth across the small space in angry strides. "If I can't kill you, what am I supposed to do with you? I can't let you go!"

Tresa sagged against the mattress, relieved she'd convinced the witch not to decapitate her.

Flannery stopped to glare at her, her calm facade gone. She dragged a hand through her hair and spoke in a low, rough voice to herself, "Think. Think. *Think*."

"I don't have to say anything to anyone," Tresa practically whispered, hoping to insinuate the idea that it would be okay to just let her go.

Flannery's eyes narrowed in thought. "I can't kill you. And I can't let you go." Then a slow smile stretched her lips.

Tresa's skin crawled. She'd obviously arrived at a solution, and if it brought a smile to Flannery's face, Tresa knew she wasn't going to like it.

Staring into Flannery's satisfied gaze, Tresa was reminded that there were fates worse than death.

DARIUS SAW SIMPSON LEAVING the station. "Hey," he called out, slamming the car door and hurrying to catch him.

Simpson looked over his shoulder, annoyance flickering across his expression when he spotted Darius. His strides increased.

Darius took a deep breath, battling to control his raging emotions. His hands flexed at his sides, opening and shutting. The beast simmered just beneath the surface, a hot slither under his skin, itching to come out.

Even if it wasn't the full moon, he was always careful to keep himself in check, but right now that control was hard won. Darius closed the distance in barely suppressed speed, falling into step beside him. "I need to talk to you. Tresa . . . she's missing. She was snatched right outside—"

Simpson shook his head. "I don't have time for this right now."

Darius grabbed his shoulder and forced

him around. The man tried to shrug free, but Darius increased the pressure of his fingers. "I think our killer took her. We need to find—"

"Look. My partner is missing." Simpson's face was tight. "In my mind, that takes precedence over some two-bit con."

"Detective Flannery?" Darius frowned.

"Yeah. She's on duty and no one has been able to get in touch with her. It's not like her. I'm going to track her down. If your girlfriend doesn't show up in seventy-two hours, come back and file a missing person report."

This time Darius let him go. He watched Simpson stalk away and get into his car and drive off. Darius stood for a moment, absorbing the fact that Flannery and Tresa were both gone. Somehow he didn't think it was coincidental. Had Flannery stumbled upon the witch's identity? Had the witch taken both the detective and Tresa captive?

With a curse, he headed for his car, his instincts bursting to the surface, determined to track Tresa down.

As he opened the door, a cold wind blew, enveloping him. He froze, scanning the landscape of cars. He squinted, peering hard. Something was there. He'd learn to trust his instincts. He could see nothing, but evil wasn't always apparent.

He watched, studied the shadows more intently. Looking beyond the still shadows cast by cars, trees, a mailbox. *There.*

A dark shadow moved swiftly. Long and narrow, it ribboned through the parking lot, weaving around a woman holding the hand of a toddler. It advanced on Darius, slithering like the living thing it was. It wrapped around him several times, coldly winding up his body.

Balthazar.

He felt the demon circle his neck, stroke his nape. Breathe into his ear. At first it just sounded like a rush of air. Wind on his face. But then he heard it. The demon's voice. Whisper soft.

Tresa . . .

Balthazar moved then, left him in a cold rush, rolling through the air and away from Darius.

Darius jumped inside the car and pulled out from his parking space in a squeal of tires. As incredible as it seemed, the dark, amorphous shape moved at a slow enough pace to follow, almost as though he was leading Darius. Guiding him.

Taking him to Tresa.

Darius wasn't fool enough to think the demon was trying to be helpful. But, for whatever reason, he wanted Darius to follow him. So Darius did.

TWENTY-FOUR

Blindfolded by a sack over her head, gagged, hands bound, Tresa stumbled along the uneven ground. Flannery's hard fingers bit into her arm, cursing her when her foot caught on something and she fell, nearly bringing Flannery down with her.

"Stupid bitch. Get up." Flannery's knife prodded into her back again. The blade against her flesh was very familiar by now. Its sharp point had cut through her shirt and blood slicked down her spine.

Tresa groaned as she was tugged to her feet. Really very clever of Flannery. The other witch knew that she had the gift to move objects—a gift that was useless when she couldn't see anything. Tresa couldn't help herself now.

"Come on. We're almost there."

The witch seemed confident that Tresa wouldn't be coming back. She strained for a sound, something, any clue to where Flannery was taking her.

Darius. She knew he'd be worried about her. These last few days together had been special. She'd even begun to hope that it was the beginning of something.

She hoped he would just go, not put himself at risk by looking for Balthazar. She could face anything, endure anything, as long as she knew he was safe.

But she would never even have that assurance.

Flannery yanked hard on her arm, pulling her to a halt. "Stop. We're here."

Even though she had already tried to throw off the sack over her head while stuffed into Flannery's trunk, she tossed her head again in an attempt to dislodge the fabric. It was no use.

"Hold still. Scoot your legs together," Flannery snapped, and then Tresa felt her hands on her legs. Abrasive rope soon followed, cutting into her calves as Flannery tied her legs together.

Without vision, all her other senses intensified. The air was chillier. She smelled trees. There was a breeze. Goose bumps broke out across her flesh.

And then she heard the barest murmur on the air. It sounded like . . . water.

Suddenly the sack was ripped from her head and she shook her hair off her face. She blinked, adjusting her eyes to the night. She stood at the edge of a bridge, suspended over a river. Water moved swiftly below.

She means to throw me in.

She gasped and staggered back.

Not again. Not again!

But the knife was still there, gouging deep, forcing her forward. Her bound arms flailed wildly as she tried to keep her balance.

Despite the fiery pain from the blade, she reared back. Falling into the river would be far worse than any knife. She couldn't drown. Not all over again. And since she couldn't die by any method other than decapitation, that meant she would drown *forever*.

Would be stuck down there, submerged . . . forever.

She cried out and arched directly into the knife's point, felt it collide with her spine. She forced her gaze wide, refusing to pass out from the pain.

The knife twisted in her back, scraping against bone.

All her concentration centered on the very spot where her nerves screamed in protest. She exerted her will, shaking from the strain of using her power. With a great gust of air, she willed the knife out of her.

"Oh no you don't!"

Flannery's hands shoved her in the shoulder blades—and then she was flying through the air.

She hit the water with a painful smack. Her body sank through the murky river water. The more her bound legs and hands thrashed, the deeper she sank. Her lungs burned. Water flooded her nose and mouth.

It was so dark she couldn't see anything around her. She could only feel. Pain. Terror. A strong wave of déjà vu swept over her, confusing her, making her wonder if she was back in the river where she'd signed over her life to Balthazar.

Only she didn't hear Balthazar's voice this time. She didn't hear anything but the rush of water around her. He wasn't coming.

No one was.

DARIUS PARKED AT THE edge of the road when the shadow vanished from the path of his headlights. A short distance away, the quiet two-lane road arched over the river. Stepping from the car, Darius followed the sound of the river, a sixth sense guiding him. The river gleamed darkly beneath the waxing light of the moon, moving swiftly, the water whispering its song.

Suddenly he glimpsed a movement on the bridge and saw Flannery, but no one else. No Tresa. And no witch. Why had Balthazar led him here?

Inhaling, he picked up Tresa's scent. She was here somewhere; she *had* to be.

Flannery started walking toward him, the steady fall of her footsteps growing closer, crunching over the gravel.

He stepped out onto the road and faced her. "Detective?"

She stopped. "Darius. What are you doing here?"

"I was going to ask you the same. I'm looking for Tresa."

She sent the barest glance over her shoulder, then quickly faced forward as if she regretted even looking. Why? He looked over her shoulder but saw nothing. No one.

"I don't know where she is," Flannery said.

And as simple as that, he knew she was lying. "What are you doing out here?"

She squared her shoulders. "I don't need to explain myself to you."

He cocked his head, remembering that Simpson had no clue as to where she was. "What about your partner? He's looking for you."

She was silent, tension radiating off her. No question about it; she was hiding something.

She looked left and right, almost as if she was looking for help. But out here in the middle of nowhere, who would be here to help her?

Sudden realization washed over him, and a curse burst from his lips. "It's *you*."

He'd never once suspected her. He was a lycan—he should know evil when face-to-face with it. But he had missed it with her and now Tresa was in trouble.

She released a small sigh. "Oh, very well. You found me out."

"Where is she?" he demanded.

She clucked her tongue as she crossed her arms. "You know, you really should have known better than to get involved with a witch . . . *lycan*."

She knew what he was. Further proof that he shouldn't underestimate her. "Where *is* she?" he repeated.

"Nowhere you can help her."

He lunged forward and grabbed her by the throat. "I'm done playing your games."

She simultaneously chuckled and wheezed. "What are you going to do? You can't kill me."

With a curse, he released her.

She gasped for breath and resumed her

laughter. "You can't help her. And you can't beat me."

He dragged both hands through his hair, wondering how he was going to get Tresa's location out of her.

She wasn't dead. He knew it. Aside from being absolutely certain that he would *feel* it if she was gone, it wouldn't have made sense for Flannery to kill her. Then she would lose Balthazar. She had to know that, too. Which meant that Flannery had stowed her away somewhere.

His gaze settled on the water, the surface rippling from the rapid current. And suddenly he knew. He *knew* Tresa was in there.

Praying he could find her, he raced down the rocky embankment and dove into the water.

Twenty-five

The agony stretched on and on. The stabbing pressure in her ears and head was excruciating. Her lungs burned, felt compressed and shriveled inside her. Her breath was gone, lost long ago. Now she simply existed beneath the water. She couldn't die this way, so she simply suffered the sensations of drowning.

Time was lost. Seconds. Minutes. Hours.

It was impossible to know.

She wished for a true death, pleaded with God to make it stop. She would go mad. There would be nothing left of her if she had to endure this much longer.

Unlike the last time, she never reached bottom. This river was deep, there was too much current. She drifted, carried along, grass and reeds stroking her as she floated.

Terror and hope mingled in her heart. Who knew where she would end up? Maybe eventually she'd wash up on a shore. Besides the pain there was the unremitting dark. So deep and penetrating it was a living thing devouring her.

The water around her suddenly stirred. Her heart rate grew wild. What else was out there? In this river with her?

Something snatched at her hair. She shrieked, the sound lost in the water. She jerked, trying to move her body away from whatever had her hair, but the tug increased. Suddenly she went tumbling back in the direction from which she was trying to escape, her bound arms pumping uselessly, trying to swim away.

Her back collided with something hard. Strong arms wrapped around her. She struggled, panicked, as she was whipped around. Then broad hands cupped her face, and she instantly recognized the way the hands held her so tenderly.

Darius.

He'd come. He'd found her.

Relief filled her, almost as sweet as the taste of air that she so desperately craved.

He swam with sure and strong strokes, holding her close as he broke through the surface, lifting her up into the air as he swam for shore. She filled her starved lungs with a sweet breath.

"It's all right," Darius gasped as he inhaled sharply, dragging her onto land with him. He wiped the wet hair back from her face as she panted and wheezed.

The sight of him, his dark, wet hair plastered to his head, the sensation of solid ground at her back—nothing was sweeter.

"Tre," he rasped, working free the ropes at her wrists and ankles with feverish speed.

She shook her head, spitting up water. "You found me."

"I'll always find you." He flashed a grin. "I think I told you that when we first met."

The sound of deliberate clapping filled the air. Tresa sat up, searching for the source.

Flannery strolled toward them, applauding leisurely. "What a dramatic rescue!" She pressed a hand to her chest. "Be still, my heart!"

Darius growled, surging to his feet.

Flannery was close enough now that Tresa could see her face. And her demon-black eyes.

She reached up and tightened her fingers around Darius's arm. "Darius, stop. It's him."

Darius looked down at her and back to Flannery.

"It's Balthazar," she murmured, standing up. The demon wore Flannery's body loosely, with none of Flannery's stiffness.

"Indeed. It's me. I couldn't leave Flannery to her own devices any longer. Things were starting to get messy. She means well, but she's young."

"Means well? She murdered five people!" Darius said.

"Like I said, she means well."

Darius's rage swelled, radiating off him like heat. Even his skin felt warmer, simmering beneath Tresa's touch.

"Good of you to follow me, lycan." Balthazar wagged a finger at him as if he were an errant child. "I tried to let my two girls here work out their differences, but they can't seem to get along."

"Work out our differences? She tried to drown me!" Tresa said.

"And you're trying to get her arrested. What good is she to me locked away in some jail cell?" The demon sighed as though pained. "Well. That's neither here or there, I suppose. I have a proposition for Darius."

Her nape tingled, her skin suddenly crawling. "Darius," she warned quietly, tugging on his arm. Balthazar's proposition would be tempting; it always was. She looked around desperately for any way out, any escape.

On the road beyond them, a lone figure strolled, a giant hiker's pack strapped to his back. A couple of cans dangled from it. He was dressed shabbily, and bearded. A hat pulled low over his face.

The cans clanked together and Balthazar's gaze followed hers. Dismissing the drifter, the demon looked back at the two of them.

"What are you offering?" Darius asked.

"Darius, don't *listen*. He—"

"Just a way to reverse your curse. Isn't that what you've been asking for?"

Her pulse skittered at her throat. Of course Balthazar knew just what to offer. The one thing Darius wanted most.

Darius's arm tensed, the muscles bunching under her grip. "You can do that?"

"Of course. I initiated your curse. I can undo it."

"Darius," she whispered. "Be careful." No one won when they played with a demon. She knew that better than anyone else.

Darius glanced down at her, and she could see in his expression that he understood her warning. This demon hadn't survived through the millennia by making mistakes.

"What's the catch?" Darius demanded, his gaze turning back to Flannery.

"Catch?" Balthazar sounded affronted.

"There's always a catch," Tresa snapped.

"Ah, well, reciprocation is only fair."

"What do you want in exchange?" Darius pressed, his handsome features harsh and unyielding in the glow of the moon.

Flannery's head cocked at a menacing angle, the movement eerie and animal-like. Then Balthazar's demon gaze swung to Tresa. "Kill her. Free me."

The words shocked through Tresa like an electrical current. She should have guessed this would be his price.

"Go to hell," Darius growled.

"Aw, I know you're fond of her, but consider it. Your curse. Ended. Mortality can be yours again. Isn't that what you want, my friend?"

"I'm not your friend."

Darius took her hand and started to lead her away.

Flannery's voice reached out, stopping them with the seductive pull of her next promise. "I meant the *entire* curse, of course. Every lycan in existence would be no more. They would be just men. Just women. Think of the lives saved . . ."

Darius stared straight ahead, his expression giving nothing away, but Tresa felt the tremor that ran through him.

The prospect of ending the curse alto-gether . . . Future generations would be saved.

She weighed the danger of one demon on the loose versus thousands of lycans. It seemed obvious.

She released Darius's hand and whirled around. "Do you mean that?" Her voice came out almost a squeak.

"Tre—"

She held up a hand to cut off whatever Darius was going to say.

"Of course I meant it. Your life, and the lycan curse is ended."

"I won't do it," Darius quickly said, forcing her around. "How could you think I would even—"

"How can you not?" she returned, her voice thick. "It's not about me." At the hot emotion swimming in his eyes, she added in a softer voice, "It's not even about us, Darius. You can save lives . . . so *many* lives."

"I can't hurt you." His breath fell raggedly. "I love you, Tre."

The words arrowed directly to her heart, painful as any wound. Because she hadn't heard them in so long. And she had never expected to hear them again.

She lifted a hand to his cheek, refusing to say the words back and make this that much harder. "You're strong. I know you can do it. You will. Because it's the right thing."

They stared at each other for a long moment.

"I'd do it to myself if I could." Her voice cracked and she swallowed. "Please, Darius. Don't make me beg."

"Please, Darius," Balthazar echoed. "Listen to her. She wants you to. If you truly love her, do as she asks. And you really would be saving so many lives. Here. You can use this. Flannery always keeps this on her." Balthazar fished out a Swiss Army knife from her pocket.

"Shut up," Darius spat, never tearing his gaze from Tresa.

Gulping down a breath, pain and sorrow wringing her heart, Tresa lifted Darius's hands to her throat. When he started to pull away, she clung all the tighter to his wrists. With his strength, it would be so easy. Just a twist of his hands.

"You can do this. You're strong." She held his horrified gaze, knowing he understood she didn't mean just physically.

Closing her eyes, she whispered, "Do it."

Inside, words whispered through her that she dared not say aloud, afraid they would stop him from doing what must be done.

I love you. I love you.

Eyes still closed, she slowly removed her hands from his and lifted her chin in offering.

Not thinking about whether it would hurt or not . . . or about what came after. If the fires of hell waited for her like she'd always believed.

She thought only of Darius. Her love for him. And the wrong she would be righting. The lives she would be saving. That would be enough.

Suddenly he wasn't touching her anymore. His hands were gone. There was a rush of wind and a sharp, grinding crunch.

By the time she opened her eyes, it was over.

TWENTY-SIX

Darius dropped the witch's head as if he held a viper. It thudded at his feet and her body followed a split second behind it. Tresa gasped, her wide eyes fixing on what was left of Flannery.

Instantly the dark shadow emerged from the fallen corpse, whirling and thickening until it took shape, became corporeal.

Darius pulled out his knife, his gaze searching, ready to find the mark of the fall and plunge it in.

He knew demons could look like anything. Still, he wasn't prepared for the sight of Balthazar. He was enormous. Tall with the muscled body of a man. Random bone-colored spikes protruded from his dark flesh. The demon flung back his head and released a triumphant roar, flexing his sinewy flesh.

Darius scanned him, desperately hunting for a glimpse of the mark. He didn't see it.

"Darius!" Tresa cried out his name. He felt her hand on his arm.

He risked a glance at her horrified face. "Get back, Tresa!"

A throaty laugh rumbled out from the demon. "Thank you for my freedom, dog." He flexed his taloned hands and stalked closer. His talons caught the moonlight, shimmering with deadly intent. "And I congratulate you on being the first victim these hands shall finally tear apart." He nodded at Tresa. "And she'll be next. I'll enjoy ripping her head from her body for all the years she's thwarted my will."

With a roar, the beast in Darius broke free and he charged, his blood burning through his veins with the violent urge to kill. To protect Tresa. Even if he stood no chance against this monster, he would fight to his last breath.

Balthazar sprang to meet him with an eerie screech. The two clashed, collided with pummeling fists and slashing claws. They writhed in a mad, twisting dance.

Pain shot through Darius and he fought through the agony, the talons shredding through his clothing into muscle and sinew. Tresa's screams penetrated the fog of pain, the sound giving him strength, and he fought harder. For her. If he fell, she was dead, too.

Suddenly Balthazar howled and arched, releasing Darius. Free, he staggered back, panting as he watched the demon twist in a circle, trying to reach behind him, groping for something that was out of his reach.

And then he saw the hilt of Flannery's Swiss Army knife sticking out from the glowing handprint on Balthazar's back. *The mark of the fall*.

Tresa stood just beyond him, her hand still poised in midair from stabbing Balthazar, a shocked expression on her face, as if she couldn't believe she had actually done it. She'd taken down the demon that had possessed her for over two thousand years and sent him straight back to hell. Pride mingled with the relief and love he felt for her.

The hideous body started to blur and turn to shadow again. The knife fell to the ground. There was no longer anything left to hold it in place.

Then Darius spotted the man he'd noticed on the road earlier. The backpacker. He stood off to the side, his shadowed face observing the mad scene.

Balthazar's shriek died away as his shadow faded. A moment more, and there was nothing but a wisp on the dark night.

Tresa moved to Darius's side and he pulled

her close, the sensation of her body against his the greatest comfort. He forgot his wounds, the pain radiating through him.

"You did it, Tresa. You're free!"

"He's gone? For good?" Tresa's voice shook with disbelief. Her eyes welled with moisture. He hugged her closer.

The stranger stepped forward and Darius and Tresa exchanged looks, unsure what to do with man who had just witnessed the unexplainable.

"Nasty creature." His voice was deep, almost melodious. "He's where he belongs now."

"And where's that?" Darius asked, starting to think this guy wasn't all he appeared to be.

"Where all demons belong. The fiery pit that gave life to him."

"Who are you?"

The man studied them, looking Darius over and then Tresa. "We've been watching you for some time."

Tresa pulled back, clearly startled. "Who is 'we'?"

Darius detected the faintest smile curve the stranger's lips. "Who are you?" he demanded.

The stranger turned his gaze on Darius, angling his head thoughtfully. "Interesting that the two of you should have found each other.

Two damned souls that should not have chased after the light." He smiled then. "But you did."

Darius's legs suddenly felt unsteady. Hope that he had never dared allow himself swelled inside him. His fingers laced with Tresa's.

The stranger continued, "Call me a *friend*. One who's fond of delivering second chances."

"Second chances?" Tresa's voice trembled with excitement. Her gaze slid to Darius, widening suddenly. "Darius!" she cried. "Your eyes!"

His hand flew to his face. "What?"

"They're not silver. They're . . . green."

Green? He knew his eyes had been green once. He could still remember his mother's green eyes and his uncle telling him his eyes were like hers.

"They're beautiful." Tresa's palm slid across his cheek tenderly. "You're free. Your curse is gone."

His hands clasped both her arms. "You're free, too."

He pulled her into his arms, hugging her so tightly he worried he was crushing her. But she didn't seem to mind. Her hands gripped his back, clutching him as though she would never let go. With no thought to their audience, they kissed like it was their first kiss. The first kiss of the rest of their lives—lives wiped clean, free of stain and soul-draining darkness.

After a moment, Darius pulled back. Remembering they weren't alone, he looked toward the stranger, but he was gone.

"Where'd he go?" Tresa whispered, scanning the area all around them.

"He's gone."

"How . . ." Her voice faded and a faint smile brushed her lips. "It doesn't matter. I'm betting we'll see him again. Someday."

His chest swelled with a weightlessness he'd never felt before. With one arm around her shoulders, he guided her toward the car. "Let's go home."

She paused, her hands smoothing over his still-wet shirt, slicking it to his chest. Her eyes gleamed up at him in the night. "Um, where is that?"

He glanced up at the waxing moon, realizing he no longer felt its pull. He wasn't a slave to it anymore. He didn't need to rush back home and lock himself up inside his prison in a week's time. He could go anywhere. The world was his. And Tresa's. They were both free to do whatever or go wherever they wished.

He lowered his head and kissed her, slow and deep. Coming up for air, he murmured against her mouth, "We'll figure that out."

EPILOGUE

Tresa opened her eyes to a bird's musical call. A slow smile spread across her face as she recalled last night. All her nights lately. She toyed with a lock of her hair and gazed up at the ceiling. The blades of a bamboo fan whirred overhead. She stretched her arms, pausing to marvel at her sun-browned skin. Morning sunlight spilled through the sheer curtains, promising another glorious day.

Rising, she slipped on the sheer robe at the foot of the bed. Tightening the sash, she strolled out to the balcony, already guessing what she would find. Darius swam with strong, steady strokes through the cerulean water, as he had every morning since they'd arrived at their island paradise. Sultry breezes, sun warm on your skin. It had always been a fantasy of hers, but now it was reality. Her reality. Hers and Darius's.

She leaned down to rest her elbows on the iron railing, watching in admiration as he emerged onto the white-sand shoreline. Her gaze roamed over his familiar form lovingly as he took the steps leading up to their balcony two at a time.

Halfway to the top his eyes alighted on her and a wide smile curved his lips. His white teeth stood out against his skin. Time in their paradise had bronzed his skin. Reaching her, he pulled her into his arms, plastering her to his wet body.

"Good morning," he murmured against her lips after a long, thorough kiss. "What do you want to do today? I was thinking breakfast . . . after a little nap, hmm?"

He pressed long, savoring kisses to the corners of her lips, her jaw, her neck. And she knew he had anything but a nap in mind.

"I don't know." Her fingers trailed across his lovely chest. "I thought we might go into Bridgetown to see a doctor."

He frowned. "Are you ill?" His body tensed and she knew the prospect worried him. They were mortal now, prone to sickness and disease. They didn't regret it for a moment—they'd fought to win back their souls—but now they faced all the vulnerabilities of humans. The most worrisome vulnerability of all was the risk of losing each other. Especially this soon. They'd just found each other.

"I'm not sick," she assured him.

Relief eased his features. "Then why . . ."

"I just think it's the thing to do."

He looked puzzled. "You mean . . . like a checkup?"

"Yeah." She tried to contain her grin. "The first of many, I'm told. Over the course of nine months."

Darius stared.

Her grin broke free. "I'm going to have a baby. *We* are."

Some of the color left Darius's face. "W-we . . . ?"

"Wow." Her fingers drummed over his chest. "I've never seen you at a loss for words."

"Tresa!" He pulled her into his arms. "How is this even possible?"

"I guess someone thought we deserved this, too. In addition to our second chance. You are glad, aren't you?"

"Glad? Glad?" He shook his head, his lips working as though he couldn't find the right words. He cupped the side of her face with his hand. "I never even dreamed of such a thing. I'd hoped for freedom from the curse, but this . . . is so much more. I have you. And now this. A part of us." He looked down as his hand moved to her stomach, where new life grew. "It's more than I could ever hope for." He lifted his gaze back to hers. "I love you."

She answered him with her lips, showing him just how much she loved him back. And how much she always would.

Love with BITE...

Bestselling Paranormal Romance
from Pocket Books!

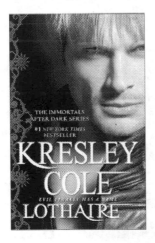

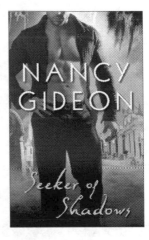

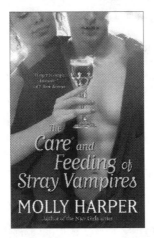

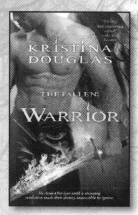
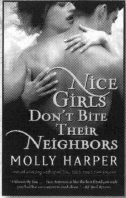

Printed in the United States
By Bookmasters